W9-BBZ-522

A primal feeling. . . .

She got no farther, for Gregory caught her by the shoulders and pulled her toward him—so close that her face was mere inches from his. He said nothing for several heart-stopping moments, merely looked at her, and Eloise was certain he meant to kiss her.

Of its own free will, the tip of her tongue moistened her lips. As Gregory watched the slow circling movement, the anger in his eyes ebbed away and something else took its place—something that made his green orbs appear darker and quite deliciously intimate, as though they searched Eloise's very soul.

No man had ever looked at her like that. The look was at once frightening and exciting—and as heat slowly engulfed her, deep inside some primal feeling sprang to life, as if it had waited a long time to be awakened by the right man.

"For the love of heaven, Eloise, think what you are doing," he said.

"I do not want to think," she said, her voice so husky it did not sound like her own. "I merely want to . . ."

An Uncommon Courtship

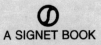

Martha Kirkland

A SIGNET BOOK

SIGNET
Published by New American Library, a division of
Penguin Putnam Inc., 375 Hudson Street,
New York, New York 10014, U.S.A.
Penguin Books Ltd, 27 Wrights Lane,
London W8 5TZ, England
Penguin Books Australia Ltd, Ringwood,
Victoria, Australia
Penguin Books Canada Ltd, 10 Alcorn Avenue,
Toronto, Ontario, Canada M4V 3B2
Penguin Books (N.Z.) Ltd, 182–190 Wairau Road,
Auckland 10, New Zealand

Penguin Books Ltd, Registered Offices:
Harmondsworth, Middlesex, England

First published by Signet, an imprint of New American Library,
a division of Penguin Putnam Inc.

First Printing, September 2000
10 9 8 7 6 5 4 3 2 1

Copyright © Martha Cotter Kirkland, 2000
All rights reserved

Ⓢ REGISTERED TRADEMARK—MARCA REGISTRADA

Printed in the United States of America

Without limiting the rights under copyright reserved above, no part of this
publication may be reproduced, stored in or introduced into a retrieval system, or transmitted, in any form, or by any means (electronic, mechanical,
photocopying, recording, or otherwise), without the prior written permission
of both the copyright owner and the above publisher of this book.

PUBLISHER'S NOTE
This is a work of fiction. Names, characters, places, and incidents either are
the product of the author's imagination or are used fictitiously, and any resem-
blance to actual persons, living or dead, business establishments, events, or
locales is entirely coincidental.

BOOKS ARE AVAILABLE AT QUANTITY DISCOUNTS WHEN USED TO PROMOTE
PRODUCTS OR SERVICES. FOR INFORMATION PLEASE WRITE TO PREMIUM MAR-
KETING DIVISION, PENGUIN PUTNAM INC., 375 HUDSON STREET, NEW YORK, NEW
YORK 10014.

If you purchased this book without a cover you should be aware that this
book is stolen property. It was reported as "unsold and destroyed" to the
publisher and neither the author nor the publisher has received any payment
for this "stripped book."

My two beautiful nieces,
Juliet and Jolie Couch Thompson.

Chapter One

Miss Eloise Kendall held two things in abhorrence—snakes and Mr. Gregory Ward—and in the space of one minute she very nearly stepped on one and was practically run down by the other. Of the two experiences, she could not decide which filled her with more loathing.

It was not enough that fate had sent a small grass snake slithering out from a break in the dry stone wall just as Eloise passed by, prompting her to hop about from one foot to the other like the veriest widgeon to keep from stepping on the greenish reptile. No, fate was not content with that singularly unpleasant encounter, for when Eloise lifted her skirts and jumped over the slithering creature, then hurried down the dusty lane in most unladylike haste, who must be driving up the lane but Gregory Ward, the one man she had hoped never to see again as long as she lived.

Wearing a stylish, white drab box coat, and looking infuriatingly calm and in command, he drove a handsome pair of chestnuts at a spanking pace. Upon spying her in agitated flight, however, he reined in the pair with a skill that brought the phaeton to an easy stop mere inches from where Eloise stood.

"You!" she said.

Had Gregory Ward been cow-handed with the ribbons, Eloise might have been less churlish in her greeting, but denied the consolation of seeing him at a disadvantage, she felt doubly gauche for having been caught running down the lane, the hem of her skirts lifted above her boot tops. The wind had played havoc with her bonnet, which was all askew, and the way her day was going, Eloise had probably given the detested man a good look at her drawers!

And not even a pair of her lace-edged drawers, but her plain, everyday cotton ones. The ones her cousin said were positively spinsterish.

Her face burning with embarrassment, Eloise dropped her skirts and straightened her bonnet. "What are *you* doing here?"

The gentleman so rudely addressed appeared almost as surprised to see Eloise as she was to see him, and he stared at her for a moment, his square, rugged face as unreadable as ever. The silent appraisal, which took in every inch of her from her shallow-crown chip straw bonnet to her brown half boots, caused heat to spread from Eloise's neck all the way to her toes. To add fuel to her fire, the detested fellow had the gall to act as though she had greeted him with utmost civility.

With a total disregard for her loathing of him, he tipped his stylish beaver hat and smiled that crooked smile she had heard a number of idiotic females refer to as "captivating." Eloise was *not* captivated.

"Miss Kendall," he drawled, "it is always a pleasure to see you. No matter when. No matter where."

Insufferable man! Must he always put her out of countenance? Remembering that she was a lady, Eloise tried for a more civil tone of voice. "What I meant to say, Mr. Ward, was that I am surprised to see you in Derbyshire at this time of year. Your usual visits to Lord Threwsbury are at Christmastime."

"Very true," Gregory Ward replied, "but my friend and I decided to stop by Threwsbury Park for a few days on our way back to London."

At the mention of the sophisticated-looking man who sat beside him, dressed from head to foot in shades of gray, the gentleman lifted his hat, revealing black curly hair that bore just the least trace of silver at the temples. A slender man, he was the very antithesis of Gregory Ward, whose light brown hair was straight as a stick and so silky it was forever falling across his broad forehead. As well, though there was not a spare ounce of flesh on Gregory's large frame, no one would ever call him slender.

"Ma'am," the gentleman in gray said.

"Sir," she replied politely.

Gregory did not introduce them; instead, he asked after the health of Eloise's cousin.

Drat the man! Why did he not drive on? Surely he could see she wished him anywhere but there. "Lady Dreighton is well, I thank you."

"And young Jeremy?"

"My brother, like most eleven-year-olds, enjoys excellent health."

"Splendid," Gregory Ward replied. "The lad continues to share a tutor with my young cousin?"

"He does."

"And the lessons? They go well, do they?"

For just an instant, Eloise thought she saw the corners of Gregory Ward's mouth twitch, and though he managed to subdue the slight movement, she could not rid herself of the suspicion that he was laughing at her.

Determined not to let him detain her for another

second, she said, "Even as we speak, Jeremy and your cousin, Basil, are at their lessons. Now, if you will excuse me, sir, I am to meet someone in the village, and I should dislike being late."

"My sources inform me," he said, detaining her further, "that you are attempting to establish a school for the village children."

Eloise was doing just that. She and the vicar had been working on the project for several months, but she did not wish to discuss with Gregory Ward something that was very dear to her heart. "The trouble with gossip, sir, is that it is spread by those whose hours are spent in idleness, and it is listened to only by those whose intellect is less than refined."

There! That should put him in his place.

"A flush hit," he said, not at all discomforted. "I collect you number me among those of less refined intellect."

"Until this moment, Mr. Ward, the refinement—or lack thereof—of your intellect had never crossed my mind."

Having delivered her parting shot, Eloise bobbed a curtsy, then turned and walked away, pleased to know that she had had the final word.

To her dismay, she heard Gregory Ward laugh aloud, and though the sound infuriated her, she continued walking, determined to ignore both him and his laughter. Apparently, her determination was not shared by a nuthatch perched on the limb of a nearby silver birch tree, for the plump little bird protested the noisy intrusion into his serenity by voicing a rather raucous *nyak-nyak*.

Eloise's sentiments exactly!

"Oh, Miss Kendall?" Gregory Ward called from just

behind her. "There is something I think you should know."

She paused, but she did not turn to look at the man. "Yes? What is it, Mr. Ward?"

"I should hate to detain you further, ma'am, especially when you are in such a great hurry, but the last time I looked, the village was in the other direction."

With that, he slapped the reins and the chestnuts sprang to immediately, passing Eloise by, then leaving her standing alone in the lane, all but choking on flying dust and mortification.

"Ohhh!" Eloise muttered, not for the first time in the past fifteen minutes. "That rude, insufferable man! It is insupportable that he is here again so soon."

Still muttering, she opened the handsome walnut entrance door of the dower house, then slammed it shut behind her with such force it threatened the panes of the numerous windows that fronted the gray stone residence. Not that Eloise cared. At that moment, the safety of the windows was of little concern to her, never mind that they gave the six front-facing rooms a delightful, picture-book view of the gentle brook that ran through much of the grounds of Deighton Hall.

Eloise was in no frame of mind to appreciate the charm of the gently flowing water, or the late summer phlox that added its sweet aroma and a touch of brilliant pink to the moss and stones on the banks of the brook. As far as she was concerned, the pretty stone footbridge her cousin's late husband had designed and had built across the clear, cool water might as well not have existed, for Eloise was blinded by her anger.

And who could blame her? That . . . that *man* had

made a fool of her once again, and in front of a stranger. "Ohhh!"

She entered the morning room and slammed that door with even greater disregard for the plaster than she had shown seconds earlier for the front windows. Her anger still smoldering, she yanked the bonnet from her head, and disregarding the fact that she had worn the pretty chapeau only once before, tossed it onto the green slipper chair beside the empty fire place.

"My dear Eloise," remarked Lady Deighton, who sat on the gold brocade settee beneath one of the front-facing windows, "I am certain you have every justification for whatever has put you in such a temper, but must you slam the doors? You startled me, causing me to stick myself with the needle, and now look at this lace. It is ruined, and you know I meant to wear this cap at the musicale."

Eloise looked at the drop of blood that stained the pretty lace confection upon which her cousin had been attaching a primrose bow knot, then to the lady herself, whose honey blond hair was arranged in a fall of ringlets that suited her still-youthful face. Only the day before, Lady Deighton had celebrated the anniversary of her birthday, but no one looking at her graceful jawline and her fresh complexion would ever guess that she was thirty-five years old.

The musicale was to be their first entertainment following a full year's mourning, and the lady had vowed with a sigh of resignation that on that occasion she absolutely *must* begin wearing caps. "And start taking my place among the dowagers."

Eloise had thought the entire idea foolish beyond permission, and reminded of it, she managed to swallow her anger, if only for a moment. "I beg your pardon, I am sure, Thea, for the ruined lace, but please do not repeat that ridiculous idea about you joining the dowagers. As for your wearing caps, I am persuaded that you should wait at least until after we have attended Lord Threwsbury's annual Christmas ball.

"After all, we have only just put away our mourning clothes for dear Lord Deighton, and we have not danced for more than a twelve-month. Surely you are entitled to enjoy one more ball before covering those pretty tresses and sitting with the chaperons."

Theadosia Deighton lifted a slender, beringed hand to her curls. "My dear Eloise, I am just vain enough to want to take your advice. That is, if you are quite certain it would not seem improper behavior in a recent widow?"

"Quite certain. Especially not in a widow as youthful as you. Besides, you are not vain."

"I am, my dear, but let us not quibble. If the truth be told, I should very much like to forgo the caps a bit longer. My only reservation is that I should hate to appear a figure of fun, like one of those females who refuses to grow old gracefully."

If Lady Deighton had hoped for further encouragement from her younger cousin, she soon realized that it was not to be, for Eloise had begun to pace the floor in some agitation. Knowing when to leave well enough alone, Thea said no more. Instead, she stuffed the detested lace cap into her workbox and shut the lid with a decided snap

"Now," she said, "suppose you tell me what has sent you home so soon, for when you set out for the village not forty minutes ago, I was quite certain you told me that you and Reverend Underwood were to take tea with Mrs. Parker-Smith and her daughter."

"Merciful heaven!" Eloise said, momentarily stopping her pacing, "I forgot all about the Parker-Smiths!"

"Forgot! My dear, how could you? You know how protective Mrs. Parker-Smith is of her hard-won social position. She sees slights even when none are intended."

"You are right, of course. She will probably never forgive me."

"In this instance, she can hardly be blamed."

Eloise sighed. "I do not blame her. It is just that the reverend and I were hoping to persuade Mrs. Parker-Smith to give us a donation for the purchase of schoolbooks."

"That is unfortunate. I would not ask her now though, if I were you. Not after forgetting her invitation."

"I dare not ask," Eloise replied, "not now."

After muttering a colorful, if rather ungenteel remark, she said, "It is all of a piece, Thea, and you may add *that* to his list of faults."

"His? Whoever do you mean?"

Eloise was too lost in thought to hear. "It is not enough that the blasted man ruins each Christmas with his visits, now he must make a shambles of my summer *and* ruin my prospects for a handsome donation."

"Blasted man? My dear, I have not the least idea who you—"

"Him," Eloise said with loathing. "The earl's nephew."

"Threwsbury's nephew? Horace Verne? Well, I admit to being surprised. Not that I blame you overmuch for disliking the fellow, for he was ever a prig and a dead bore, but—"

"Not Lord Verne. The other one. Ward."

"One of the Wards? Surely you do not mean *Gregory* Ward?"

When Eloise made no demur, Thea said, "But, my dear, Gregory is received everywhere. Excellent *ton*. Of course, he is a rascal, to be sure, but such a charming one. And so tall and han—"

"Charming! How can you say so? Why, the man is an overbearing, pompous, conceited boor!"

Thea blinked in surprise. "Such heat, my dear. What on earth has he done to make you take him in such dislike?"

Unable to withstand the many memories that flooded her brain, Eloise returned to pacing the room. How did one explain such aversion?

"For my part," Thea continued, "I confess to a soft spot in my heart for the dear boy."

"Boy! If he is a boy, then I am still a schoolroom chit. He is thirty if he is a day! A full six years older than me."

"Oh?" Thea said, giving her cousin a speculative look. "How come you to know his exact age?"

Eloise stopped short, unsure how to answer that without revealing more than she wished. "When I was six years old, Mother and I attended his birthday party."

"Of course. I had forgotten that Kendall Grange and Wardly House were both situated rather near Stoke-On-Trent. Naturally your parents would know Sir Cecil and Lady Ward. And you must have known both their sons quite well."

Far too well! "The older son, who is Sir Cecil's heir, I know only slightly, for he was already up at Oxford at that time. It is Gregory I know far better than I wish. The big oaf!"

Eloise missed the look of growing interest in her cousin's eyes, for she was busy removing the apricot-colored kid gloves that perfectly matched her spencer. Having reached the mature age of four-and-twenty, and being blessed with dark brown hair and equally dark brown eyes, Eloise had abandoned the pastels and whites favored by young, unmarried girls, and following the mourning period for her cousin's husband, had begun wearing brighter, more vivid colors.

Thea watched with fascination as Eloise slapped the kid gloves across her open palm, almost as if she were imagining the palm was someone's face, and she was challenging that someone to a duel. "I had a pretty lace dress with a pink pinafore," Eloise began without preamble, "and he ruined it."

Thankfully for Thea's composure, she realized the *ruined* dress—having been described as possessing a pinafore—must have been worn to the child's birthday party. Gregory Ward had a well-deserved reputation with the ladies, but his inamoratas were always high flyers and dashing widows; Thea could not recall ever seeing him go beyond the line with an unmarried girl.

No one who knew Theadosia Deighton would call her a slowtop, and though she was not as bookish as her young cousin—who was dangerously close to being thought *blue*—she knew the beginning of a good story when she heard one, and she was not about to let this one get by. "I collect," she said, "that the dress was ruined at the birthday party. You were six, I believe you said."

"Yes. And that great, lumbering oaf had just turned twelve."

"Gregory, do you mean?"

"Do you know another such person?"

Among Thea's acquaintances there were three or

four gentlemen she would readily consign to the ranks of oaf, but Lord Threwsbury's nephew was not among their number. Gregory Ward was at least six feet tall, and quite muscular, with the broad back and thick neck of the devoted athlete, but Thea had danced with him on more than one occasion, and she could attest to the fact that though he was powerfully built, he was as graceful as a cat.

"I will admit," she said, "that the gentleman's chin is a bit stubborn. And, if I were obliged to describe him, I would say his features were too rugged for any true pretension to masculine beauty, but oh, when he smiles that crooked smile—"

"Not you, too, Thea? And you a respectable widow."

"Must a widow pretend to be blind?"

"Not at all."

"Then allow me to tell you, Eloise, that I *adore* Gregory's smile. As for his manners, I find them both polished and appealing. Too appealing, perhaps, for rumor has it that he once—" Aghast at what she had been about to relate, Thea said, "Your pardon, Eloise, but what I was about to say is not fit for the ears of an unmarried female."

"That I can believe! Not that I have the least interest in hearing gossip about Gregory Ward's peccadilloes."

"His indiscretions not withstanding, I doubt you could find another person in the entire country who would share your obvious dislike of Gregory Ward. He is universally liked."

"Others do not know him as I do."

Since Thea was agog to know just *how* well her cousin knew the gentleman in question, she kept any further opinions to herself, choosing instead to bid

Eloise continue with her story. "A lace dress," she prompted, "with a pink pinafore."

"It was beautiful," Eloise began. "Mother had purchased it while in London, and Father said I looked like a fairy princess in it. I do not think I have ever loved a dress more."

"So you wore it to the birthday party at Wardly House?"

"Yes. I was really too young to attend a party for a boy who was already at school, but the neighborhood was scarce of suitable children, so Lady Ward invited Mother and me to help fill the numbers."

"A practice that is so often necessary," Thea said, commiserating with any hostess who must make up a proper party in a neighborhood where acceptable families are few and far between.

"As luck would have it," Eloise continued, "two of Gregory's school chums from Harrow were there as well, and if I ever saw a pair who were gallows-bound, those two boys fit the bill. They had run about the house like a pair of wild savages, disrupting the party and even knocking over a priceless Sevres shepherdess, so in desperation Lady Ward ordered the party moved outside, to a Grecian folly built some fifty years earlier, near a shallow pond."

"Oh, dear. A pond, you say?"

"Exactly," Eloise replied. "And to make matters worse, the folly, the pond, and a small boat dock, had all been allowed to fall into disrepair. A yellowish green scum lay on top of the water, and tall, thick reeds grew all along the banks—reeds that were alive with croaking frogs and who knows what else." After a shudder of distaste, she said, "I am persuaded you can guess the rest."

"I can, but I should much prefer to hear it from you. Pray, continue with your story."

Not at all reluctant to do so, Eloise said, "Gregory's two friends must have found the party dull fare, for they began to nose about for some adventure. Unfortunately, they discovered an old punt abandoned beneath a willow tree that overhung the edge of the pond. The pole used for maneuvering in the shallow water was still lashed to the side of the narrow, flat-bottomed boat, so the boys climbed into the punt and began arguing straight away about who should have the first turn as captain of the vessel."

"And what of the birthday boy? Where had he been all this time?"

Eloise shrugged. "I have no idea. I had been picking a bouquet of heart's ease to give my mother, taking care not to get too near the reeds with their watery mud and croaking frogs, and I paused only when I heard the pair from Harrow begin to argue. Gregory seemed to appear from nowhere, just in time to grab the end of the punt and stop his friends from going out onto the pond.

" 'It will not float,' he told them. 'Best to get out now, before it begins to take on water.'

" 'Spoil sport,' both boys replied."

"Little devils," Thea said. "Did they heed his warning?"

"They disregarded it entirely, and when they moved as if they meant to go out anyway, Gregory grabbed the pole. Naturally, his friends refused to give over, declaring it to be their right as the discoverers of the craft to have a go at poling it."

Eloise's full lips were pursed in remembered anger, and fearing she might not finish the story, Thea said, "What happened? Did the punt go down?"

"*It* did not," she said, "but *I* did!"

Thea was obliged to bite down hard on her bottom lip to keep from smiling.

Unaware of her cousin's growing amusement, Eloise continued. "Both Gregory's friends jumped him at once, grabbing the pole in an attempt to take it from him. He being such a big boy for his age, not to mention a member of the school's Greco-Roman wrestling team, his friends were unsuccessful."

"The wrestling team, eh? That accounts for his rather muscular neck. I have often thought he must find the fashionably high shirt points exceedingly uncomfortable and—"

"Thea! We were not discussing Gregory Ward's neck!"

"Of course not, my love. Pray go on with your story. What happened once the boys tried to wrest the pole from their host?"

Eloise drew a deep breath to calm her emotions, though it was not perfectly clear whether she was more annoyed with her cousin's interruption or with the memory of the events at the pond. "As I was saying, the two boys from Harrow struggled with all their might, but Gregory merely laughed at their attempts, as if it was all a big joke. He had backed away, obliging his opponents to step out of the punt into ankle-deep muddy water, and one of them slipped in the mud and fell, letting go of the pole."

"Good for Gregory."

"*Humph!*" Eloise said, not sharing her cousin's opinion. "I suppose he meant to shake the other boy loose as well, for Gregory planted his feet wide apart and gave the pole a mighty twist, turning his body as he did so. Unfortunately, the boy must have discerned

Gregory's intention, and not wanting to follow his friend into the mud, he let go his hold just in time."

"And," Thea prompted.

"Naturally, with both the opponents gone, the pole was suddenly light, and as Gregory continued to swing around, with nothing to stop his momentum, he made a full circle—a circle that included the spot of ground on which I stood, still clutching the bouquet of freshly picked heart's ease."

Thea only just smothered a chuckle. "Oh, dear. Poor Eloise. What happened next?"

Eloise gave her cousin a withering look. "Surely you can guess. As that great oaf swung the pole around, it hit me in the middle of the back, knocking the breath from my body and sending me flying. I landed in the reeds at water's edge, and when I tried to get up, to escape from the ooze and any lurking slimy creatures, I slipped in the mud and fell once again. Only this time I landed facedown in the pond."

Recalling the moment all too vividly, Eloise shivered. "It was awful. Filthy water rushed up my nose, and while I flailed about, trying desperately to get my head above water so I could breathe, he caught me around the waist and lifted me out of the pond."

"He? Are you telling me it was Gregory who pulled you out?"

"Of course."

"Why, how heroic."

"Heroic? No such thing! For it was Gregory who knocked me in."

"Yes, but—"

"There was I, gasping for air, my nose and mouth full of stagnant water, and my beautiful new dress covered in mud and yellow-green pond scum, and what does that imbecile do but toss me over his shoulder like a sack of potatoes and run up to the folly, where he laid me facedown on the grass."

When she paused, Thea said, "For the love of heaven, do not stop there. What happened after he rescued—I mean, after he laid you down upon the grass?"

"I could hear my mother crying from someplace close by. There were other voices as well—excited voices—for everyone had gathered around as though I were some raree-show. While they all watched, not lifting a finger to help me, that oaf straddled me like I was a pony and began to press his hands on my back, counting all the while, *one two lift, one two lift, one two lift.*"

"What happened next?"

"What do you think happened, with him mauling me about, pushing on my back then lifting up on my ribs? I retched up my dinner and half the pond. I have never been so embarrassed in my entire life!"

It was fortunate for Lady Deighton's composure, and the further harmony of the relationship between the cousins, that the story was interrupted at that moment by the entrance of Master Jeremy Kendall.

"I say," the lad began, "what have I missed?"

"Nothing," his sister replied.

"I must have missed something, for Cousin Thea seems ready to burst from holding in her laughter, while you look as though you are ready to do murder."

"Your sister was just telling me a story about something that happened—"

"Never mind," Eloise said. " 'Tis a long story, and one I do not care to repeat."

"Not fair," the boy said, "I never get to hear the good stuff."

Jeremy Kendall was a smaller, scruffier version of his sister; like her, slender with dark brown hair and dark eyes. Where his sister was neat as a pin, however, the boy seemed always to need his hair combed away from his face and his shirt tucked back into his nankeens. Though he went out each morning suitably scrubbed and combed and with his clothes neatly pressed, as often as not when he returned in the evening, some article of his clothing wanted mending and he had gained some new minor wound on his elbows or his knees.

A good boy for all that, he was devoted to his sister, and like her, unfailingly grateful to their cousin for having given them a home three years ago when their parents perished from the influenza. Knowing better than to take a seat on Lady Deighton's furniture, Jeremy plopped down on the carpet, leaning his back against the end of the settee.

"Oh, my," Thea said after sniffing the air around him once or twice, "you do smell ripe, Jeremy. Might one ask where you have been?"

"Fishing," the boy replied. "Mr. Browne had the headache, so he asked Basil and me if we would like a day off from our lessons. Naturally, we said we would, and fearing that Lord Threwsbury might come along and revoke our unexpected holiday, or make us take along one of the footmen, we played least in sight, grabbed up rods and reels, and made a bee line for the weir."

Jutting his chest out in justifiable pride, he said, "I caught a pair of brown trout, while Basil landed only a rather small stone loach. I gave the trout to Cook, and she means to serve them for dinner. I might have caught more, but we had to stop early. Basil got a bit too close to the edge of the bank, missed his footing, and fell headfirst into the water."

Thea almost choked. "Fell into the water, you say? How . . . how unfortunate. Tell me, was Mr. Gregory Ward anywhere close by?"

"Thea!"

"Mr. Ward? Why, no, there was just the two of—" Jeremy paused, obviously at a loss to understand why his sister should go all red in the face, or what had sent his cousin into whoops over a fellow taking an unexpected dunking.

Chapter Two

Though Lady Deighton had found the story of Basil's unplanned swim in the water at the weir quite diverting, coming as it did upon the heels of Eloise's tale of falling in the pond at Wardly House, amusement was far from the reaction of the inhabitants of the neighboring estate. One at least of the males assembled in the library at Threwsbury Park thought the lad's dunking a matter of some seriousness.

"He might have drowned!" the unlucky fisherman's grandfather yelled to his butler. "Light a fire, then send for Greeley, I want the boy out of those wet clothes immediately, before he takes a chill and succumbs to a putrid sore throat."

To say the earl was overprotective of his ten-year-old grandson was to understate the matter. For his part, Lord Threwsbury considered young Basil his heir. His younger son, the boy's father, had been killed in a riding accident, and as for his lordship's older son, no one knew if Justin was alive or dead, for he was on an archeological dig in Persia and had not been heard from for a twelve-month.

Part of the silver-haired gentleman's overcautiousness regarding his grandson's health was a result of his own way of life. Having lived the last fifty of his seventy-five years as a hypochondriac, the earl looked upon Basil's every head cold as an occasion to call in the physician. As for the cuts and scrapes that are so much a part of every boy's experience, those the earl considered nothing less than threats upon his grandson's life.

That Lord Threwsbury was entertaining his favorite nephew, who had only just arrived in company with a gentleman from London, weighed not at all with their host. As far as his lordship was concerned, the world must stop until his grandson was saved from any possible repercussions following a tumble into the cool, clean water at the weir.

Though Mr. Gregory Ward did not approve of his uncle's excessive protectiveness, thinking it might prompt young Basil to fancy himself frail, he kept his tongue between his teeth upon the subject. *He* had not been made the boy's guardian, the earl had, and so long as the lad was not wholly ruined by the immoderate amount of cosseting he received, there was nothing Gregory could say. Basil would be going to school next year, along with his neighbor, the Kendall lad, and Gregory knew from experience that the boys would not be cosseted once they got to Harrow.

As soon as Lord Threwsbury, along with at least five of his male servants, escorted the boy to the safety of his room, Gregory turned to the gentleman who sat opposite him on one of the room's comfortable green leather sofas. "Your pardon, I am sure, Colin, for this veritable tempest in a teapot."

The gentleman with the dark, curly hair returned his cup and saucer to a small table to his right, then he crossed one slender gray-clad leg over the other. "Think nothing of it. One makes allowances for doting grandparents." He smiled then, and rubbed his forefinger across his neatly trimmed black mustache. "Especially when one hopes to wrest campaign funds from said doting grandparent."

Still quite new to politics, Gregory did not know whether to smile at the gentleman's remark or wish himself elsewhere. If the truth be known, Gregory would have preferred to bankroll his own campaign, but it seemed that was not the way things were done. Gaining pledges of support—both financial and emotional—was the way of politics, and because Gregory embraced an agenda of reforms that could only be approached through the Houses of Parliament, he had determined to do what it took to get elected the Member from his district. To that end, he was allowing himself to be advised by Mr. Colin Jamison, the Whig party whip and a very knowing fellow.

Only just turned forty, Mr. Jamison was as smart as he could stare, and for a younger son of an obscure North Country squire, he had accomplished a great deal in both the social and the political arenas. Respected by Whig and Tory alike, he was also the darling of the London political hostesses, who admired his classically handsome profile, his rich baritone singing voice, and his impeccable taste and savoir faire.

Though he had adopted the habit of wearing only shades of gray during the daylight hours, the sartorial idiosyncrasy had merely added to his reputation for elegance, an elegance that was exceeded only by his keen political sagacity.

To Gregory, who loved all things physical, Colin Jamison had but one flaw, his dislike of any activity that encouraged sweat. Still, Gregory could not help but admire the gentleman for what he had already achieved in his life, and the two men, who had formed an instant rapport, were fast becoming friends.

"What say you," Mr. Jamison began, "to shaking a few hands and making ourselves generally agreeable while we are in the neighborhood? You have friends here in Derbyshire, and there might be some among them who would be pleased to support your campaign."

Before Gregory could reply, Colin said, "What of the young lady we met in the lane? You called her *Miss* Kendall. Has she a father or an older brother? Perhaps they, or the lady herself, might wish to make a contribution."

A chuckle was Gregory's initial response. "I doubt the lady would be so inclined."

"Oh? Short of funds, is she?"

"I am not privy to her financial situation. Her father is deceased, and though I believe he left his two children with a modestly comfortable inheritance, I cannot think Miss Eloise Kendall would wish to contribute any of it to my future. If I were to hazard a guess, I would say that the lady—were she an heiress to a considerable fortune—would not spare me so much as a groat if I were lying in the lane, about to perish for want of food."

"Oh, ho! I thought she was in a bit of a hurry to be on her way. She does not, then, number among your rather impressive list of female admirers?"

Gregory vouchsafed no response to that question; instead, he said, "I pulled her out of a pond once, years ago, a pond in which she very nearly drowned."

"Well, now," Colin said, "surely she was appreciative of your heroic—"

"Appreciative? As soon as she had disgorged all the pond water she had drunk, the little spitfire struggled to her feet and kicked me in the shins."

Colin Jamison laughed. "An odd display of gratitude, to be sure."

"Not at all, considering the fact that it was I who

pushed her into the water in the first place. Quite by accident, of course."

"You said it happened years ago. Did time not heal the breach?"

"It did not. Furthermore, our next encounter only added to the young lady's feelings of ill-usage."

"What did you do this time? Pull her from a burning building?"

"Something far worse. I asked her to dance with me."

"Continue," bid the gentleman in gray, "for you find me quite at a loss to understand why an invitation to dance should instill further animosity."

"First," Gregory began, "you must understand my circumstances when next I saw the feisty little girl who had assaulted my shinbones. At least, I supposed it to be the next time. She had changed so much I almost did not recognize her, and I might well have passed her by in the intervening years without knowing who she was."

"A beauty, was she?"

Gregory shook his head. "Not then. Of course, she had been a pretty little girl, with thick, dusky ringlets and big brown eyes, but where some young ladies are lovely at sixteen, Eloise Kendall still had that coltish look. Her face was comely enough, I suppose, but like many a schoolroom chit, though she had gained her height, she was still quite thin, with only the promise of the figure to come."

"Your circumstances," Colin prompted. "You said I must understand them."

"Right. It was Christmas of the first year after I had completed my course at Oxford, and like so many young sprigs just let loose on the town, I thought I owned the world. A young man of family and fortune,

I was accepted in all the most fashionable salons and received invitations from all the best families. As well, my proficiency at Manton's and Jackson's assured my welcome for all manner of gentleman's pursuits."

"Quite understandable," Colin said.

"Understandable or not, I am obliged to admit that my rapid social success turned me into a bit of an ass. I had even begun a liaison with a woman ten years my senior—a beautiful creature whose husband spent too much time at the gaming hells and too little time with his wife—and as a result of that liaison, I thought myself unbelievably suave and debonair."

Mr. Jamison smoothed his mustache in an attempt to hide his smile. "Let me guess. Miss Kendall, when you met her again, did not share your view of your newly won polish."

"As always, my dear Colin, you have made short work of getting to the heart of the matter. Would that I had possessed a bit of your perspicacity. Alas, when I accompanied my brother and my new sister-in-law to the Christmas assembly at the subscription rooms at Stoke-On-Trent I behaved like the dolt I was."

"What did you do? Strut around the room like a peacock, allowing the gathered rustics to admire your newly acquired town bronze?"

Gregory laughed. "Acquit me of that, at least. Though I was quite puffed up in my own conceit, I contented myself with holding up the wall in what I was certain was a pose worthy of Lord Byron himself. Like that poetic gentleman, I had adopted the quizzing glass as part of my costume, and I was confident that it lent me just the right air of jaded boredom. When I employed the glass to survey the room, I chanced to spy Eloise Kendall, who sat along the wall with her mother and two or three other youngish girls whose hands had not been solicited for the next set."

"Ah," Colin said, "here it comes. You asked her to dance. Very gallant of you."

"Not at all, I assure you. She was merely the only female I knew by name. Thinking to give the poor girl a treat, I sauntered over to the row of chaperons and wallflowers, and after bowing with all my new-found grace, I condescended to ask the coltish Eloise if she would like to join the set that was forming?"

"And her reply?"

"She turned as pink as the tiny rosebuds that adorned her simple georgette gown, but at her mother's urging she finally placed her hand in mine."

Mr. Jamison availed himself of the cup he had abandoned moments earlier and sipped at the fragrant tea. "So far, my friend, the experience sounds quite unexceptionable."

"Yes," Gregory agreed, "but up to that point the young lady had remained seated. Only when she rose did I realize that I stood on the hem of her gown."

Colin rolled his eyes heavenward. "Tell me you did not ruin the young lady's hem."

"Ruin her hem? Oh, no. That would have been forgivable, for such mishaps occur all the time. What I did went far beyond that sort of faux pas."

Gregory glanced at his booted feet, as if he still could not believe they had played him false. "Miss Kendall had taken no more than a step or two when I heard the unmistakable sound of ripping silk. At first I could not imagine where the sound had come from, for it seemed to go on forever, then the poor young lady whipped around. For an instant she stared at me, resignation and incredulity warring for dominance in her eyes, but after a moment, her gaze went to what appeared to be the entire back of her skirt, which now lay on the floor at my feet."

Mr. Jamison could no longer suppress his laughter. "Did she kick your shins again?"

"I only wish she had. Her face went ashen, and while I tried to apologize, she bent and retrieved her skirt. Or rather, she tried to retrieve it, but was obliged to give it a tug to remind me to move my big feet. Then, holding the torn length of silk behind her to shield her shift from the prying eyes of at least fifty curious onlookers, she walked across the dance floor toward the door, her mother in pursuit."

Gregory sighed. "At that moment, I had no idea which one of us was more embarrassed. However, as I watched that coltish chit leave the assembly room, her dress in ruins but her head held as high as a queen's, I knew which one of us deserved to be embarrassed, and it was not Eloise Kendall."

Gregory said no more, and for several moments he was lost in remembered remorse. He had acted like an ass, and a young, unsophisticated girl had paid the price. He had written to her, of course, apologizing for the incident, but the reply to his letter came not from Eloise but from her mother.

The next time he and Eloise Kendall met was at Almack's, London's holiest of holies, also known as "The Marriage Mart." It was the Season of Eloise's come-out, and Gregory was on recuperative leave from his cavalry regiment, having sustained a wound to the shoulder in a skirmish just prior to Waterloo.

Four years had passed since his and Eloise's last meeting, and when he saw her, surrounded by a small group of admiring young men, all of whom were vying for the chance to partner her in a dance, or procure her a cup of Negus, Gregory could not believe the testimony of his eyes. Time had transformed the colt-ish girl he remembered into a beautiful young woman with fiery brown eyes and full luscious lips.

Because he suffered under the totally unfounded belief that enough time had passed for the young lady to view their previous meetings as occasions for humor, he made his way across the room, stopping just in front of her. Since the entire town looked upon Gregory as something of a hero, he felt certain her swains would not begrudge him a dance with the lovely Eloise.

As he suspected, the young men gave way. To Greg-ory's surprise, however, when he bowed politely, then solicited Eloise Kendall's hand in the next dance, she turned her back to him, giving him the cut direct.

Following the gasps of surprise, the ballroom was suddenly quiet enough to hear the proverbial pin drop. All eyes were on the small group of swains and the young lady who had turned her back on the town's current hero.

For his part, Gregory understood Eloise's senti-ments, and he accepted the snub without rancor. Unfor-tunately, the *ton* viewed her actions as unforgiveably pert, and no matter how many times he explained the situation to those who would listen, the damage was already done.

Within the week, her voucher for Almack's was re-scinded, and for the remainder of the Season all the best hostesses dropped Eloise Kendall's name from their lists of party guests. Her come-out was ruined.

That uncomfortable recollection was interrupted by the return of the earl's ancient butler, who announced that the gentlemen's rooms were ready. "His lordship sends his apologies for his continued absence, but he bids you both join him in the small drawing room at half past five for a predinner sherry."

The earl kept country hours, and even though his daughter-in-law, young Basil's mother, was spending a month with her sisters at Bath, leaving the gentlemen without the benefit of a hostess, dinner was still a formal affair consisting of three courses and numerous removes. The meal lasted fully two and a half hours, but the time was well spent, for the conversation was mostly political, with much of it concerning the massacre that had occurred a fortnight earlier at St. Peter's Fields in Manchester.

"Six hundred wounded," the earl said, "and a dozen dead."

"Actually, Uncle, the numbers have been reported out of all proportion, but that is not to say that the attack by sword-wielding yeomanry upon a crowd of unarmed citizens was not both tragic and despicable. Of course, the initial stupidity of 'Peterloo,' as it is being called, was in sending those ill-trained, nervous troops to disburse the crowd."

"Damnation, lad!" his uncle shouted, "peace must be maintained."

"Must it?" Gregory asked quietly. "No matter the costs?"

"Of course it must!"

"Then by whose words do we define peace? Or rebellion, for that matter. Surely, sir, you do not deny that reforms are sorely needed. Only look at the veterans of Waterloo, many of whom are now homeless and jobless. After all this time, thousands of those men are still waiting for some show of appreciation from the nation they defended."

The earl made a *humph* sound. "Worthless vagabonds the lot of them. Last month a small band of so-called veterans were apprehended not ten miles from here, near Creswell Crags. They were holed up in some of the caves, supporting themselves by stealing livestock and poultry from honest farmers, and by waylaying unsuspecting travelers on the road."

The old gentleman pounded his fist on the table, causing the ornate silvery cutlery to rattle. "Believe me, if I were ten years younger, I would show the scoundrels *my* appreciation. I would deport the lot of them to a penal colony. Give 'em a taste of real hardship."

Gregory had heard this argument too many times before to dignify it with a reply. True, a small percentage of the veterans had taken to a life of crime, but most of them were law-abiding men merely trying to support their families in a world that was changing too fast for them to keep pace.

"All I know," he said quietly, "is that life can be hard for those who must work to survive; especially in this new, mechanized world where men are being replaced right and left by machinery. I do not think it is asking too much, Uncle, that we, the privileged few who come into this world hosed and shod, do something every now and then to make life a bit easier for the less fortunate."

"What is this?" the earl demanded. "I thought you were a Whig. You sound like one of those damned Ludites!"

Gregory shook his head. "Not at all, sir. I am in favor of the progress made in both science and machinery. Furthermore, I am a Whig to the core. But even a Whig can see an injustice and wish to right it."

The conversation that followed was less heated, and while the gentlemen sat at table, enjoying their port and cigars, Mr. Jamison asked for and received a rather substantial campaign pledge from Lord Threwsbury. Along with the promised money came a suggestion that the party whip consult his lordship's neighbor, Lady Deighton, for the names of those of the local gentry who might be willing to lend their support to Gregory Ward in his bid to become a Member of Parliament.

"Theadosia Deighton is no longer lady of the manner," the earl said, "having turned over the keys to the new heir's wife, but she still figures as the leading hostess in the neighborhood. She will know better than I whose acquaintance you should seek."

Mr. Jamison readily accepted the suggestion. Having been reared by his paternal grandmother, he had a soft spot in his heart for elderly ladies, and he was quite willing to make himself agreeable to the earl's friend, the dowager Lady Deighton. "What say you, Gregory? Shall we pay a call on the old girl tomorrow?"

Gregory schooled his countenance, not allowing his amusement to show. He had remained noticeably quiet during the latter portion of the conversation, choosing to take no part in the appeal for funds, but he offered no resistance to the suggestion that they visit the ladies at the dower house on the morrow. In fact, he rather looked forward to the event, if for no other reason than to see the expression on Colin's face when he met the "dowager."

The following day dawned sunny and warm, and even though the distance between the entrances to the two adjoining estates was little more than a mile, an easy walk in such balmy weather, the ever-punctilious Mr. Jamison would not hear of presenting himself in Lady Deighton's drawing room all dusty from the road. "Trust me in this," he said, "elderly ladies put special emphasis on such niceties."

Keeping his face unreadable, Gregory ordered the chestnuts put to the phaeton, and just at noon, the gentlemen arrived at the dower house. They were invited into the vestibule by a plump, rosy-cheeked maid who then hurried to scratch at a door to the right.

"My lady," the servant said, "you've visitors. Mr. Ward and a Mr. Jamison. You want I should show them in?"

"By all means," came the reply.

Permission granted, the servant stood aside to allow the gentlemen entrance to the morning room. "This way, if you please, sirs."

It was a cheerful room, the wallpaper done in soft yellow rosebuds above mellowed oak wainscotting, but for all the attention the gentleman in gray gave his surroundings, he might just as well have been ushered into a stable. The usually imperturbable Mr. Jamison had eyes for nothing and no one but the slender, golden-haired lady who had set a fashion periodical on the table and was now rising to greet her guests.

As for the party whip's celebrated silver tongue, it seemed to have deserted him at first sight of the vision in lavender-blue zephyr gingham.

"My dear Gregory," their hostess said, crossing the muted gold-and-tan carpet to give him her hand. "I heard you were in town, and I am so glad you stopped by. What a delight to see you."

"Lady Deighton," Gregory said, bowing over the proffered hand, "the delight is all mine, I assure you." Then, "May I present my friend, Mr. Colin Jamison? He was desirous of making your acquaintance."

"Oh?" Thea said, turning the full force of her pretty blue eyes upon the stranger.

No longer able to contain his amusement, Gregory chuckled at his friend's expense. "What was it you said last evening, Colin, about wanting to pay a call upon the old g—"

"Ma'am," Mr. Jamison interjected rather abruptly, finding his voice at last, "it is kind of you to receive us."

"Not at all, sir. You are most welcome."

Motioning toward a green slipper chair beside the fireplace, she invited Mr. Jamison to be seated. Then, after disposing herself upon the settee and patting the cushion beside her, she said, "Gregory, come sit next to me. I want to hear the latest *on dits* from town, and I am persuaded that you are just the man who will know them all."

Colin took the chair the lady offered, but for the next few minutes he said nothing, allowing the two old acquaintances to bring one another up to date on news of family and friends. Not that Colin heard anything of what was said. The words were spoken in English, he was reasonably certain of that, but he had trouble understanding them.

He was bemused. Stunned. "Pixilated," his north country grandmother would have called him.

From the moment he set eyes upon the dowager Lady Deighton, Colin knew exactly how a man would feel after being kicked in the head by a horse. In his entire life, he had never seen a more perfect creature than Theadosia Deighton. Accustomed to the plump cheeks and vapid stares of the young females presented for his notice each Season at Almack's, Colin was unprepared for the loveliness of the lady before him. No longer a girl, here was a woman in her full beauty, and it was enough for Colin merely to look at her, she with her golden curls and her sweet smile.

"We can stay in the neighborhood only a few days," he heard Gregory say, "for Colin and I must be in London no later than Monday. I have been invited for a private meeting with the Prime Minister."

"A meeting with Lord Liverpool?" the lady said. "Why, Gregory, how marvelous for you. I do not claim to know all that much about politics, but I should think such a meeting would be a singular honor."

For Colin's part, he had been pleasantly surprised to discover that the lady even knew the Prime Minister's name. Most females gave little thought to politics or politicians. Not that he blamed them overmuch. In all fairness, it took an exceptional female to show an interest in a system in which she was legally barred from participating.

"It is most definitely an honor," Gregory agreed. "As you can imagine, Liverpool's support is crucial to my success in politics, and if I am to have a positive effect as a representative of my constituents, I cannot let anything prevent me from attending that meeting."

"Of course you cannot," their hostess agreed.

She smiled, then placed her finger on her chin in a playfully dramatic manner, as though studying him. "Let me see," she said, "if I can guess your party affiliation. Tory or Whig?"

When Gregory drew breath to speak, she waved him to silence. "No, no. Do not tell me, for I think I know. You are . . ." After another moment's deliberation, she said, "You are not a Tory, but will be a member of the loyal opposition."

"Very good," Gregory replied.

"And you, Mr. Jamison?" she said, turning toward Colin, the smile still in her eyes. "Are you a Whig as well?"

Gregory answered for him. "Colin is a most important Whig, for he is the party whip."

"Is he now? How very interesting."

Colin just stopped himself from asking her if she knew what that was, and in the next moment, he thanked his lucky stars for keeping him silent.

"My father never missed a political rally in our neighborhood," Lady Deighton informed them, "and I sometimes accompanied him. Once he took me to hear a speech given by Mr. Clive Smithers, unquestionably the most persuasive Tory whip of all time, and for the remainder of that summer I wore my heart on my sleeve for that very distinguished gentleman." She smiled to show that she was in jest. "Of course, that was before I met my late husband."

When she looked directly at Colin, he found he had trouble drawing sufficient breath into his lungs, and he decided it was as well for his future that both the lady's husband and the eighty-year-old Smithers had gone to their final reward. Had it not been so, the present party whip might have been forced to challenge both men to a duel for having captured the heart of Theadosia Deighton.

She was everything Colin had ever wanted, but had decided he was destined never to find. Forty years a bachelor, he could not believe his good fortune in coming to Mansfield Downs, for here was the lady of his dreams. Gifted with both beauty and charm, she possessed as well an extraordinary knowledge of politics. And to add to these virtues, she was no longer wed!

As he gazed at the lady, who had resumed her conversation with Gregory, Colin Jamison searched his brain to discover what he had done to prompt heaven to reward him in this way. He could remember no act of his that deserved such recompense, but under no circumstances would he turn his back on this unlooked-for stroke of good luck.

Carpe diem had been his motto from early childhood, and he meant to seize this opportunity with both hands. Before the week was over, and he was obliged to return to London for a meeting of his own with the Prime Minister, Colin Jamison meant to have fixed his interest with the lovely Theadosia Deighton.

Chapter Three

Unaware that her matrimonial fate had been sealed, Thea glanced toward the slender gentleman dressed in gray. He was smiling and rubbing his forefinger across his mustache, as though he had just recalled a secret, one that brought him a great deal of pleasure. Thea mistrusted that smile.

From the moment the handsome fellow had entered the room, he had watched her every move—regarding her as a man regards a woman. Having been married thirteen years, and widowed for a twelve-month, Thea had almost forgotten how it felt to be looked at in that way. *Almost* forgotten.

As much as civility would allow, she had tried to ignore the gentleman, keeping the conversation going between herself and Gregory Ward, but she had felt Mr. Jamison's gaze upon her . . . could feel it still. His dark eyes seemed to be looking deep within her soul; probing, examining, seeking answers to questions she had not been asked.

Or had she?

She looked away quickly, unwilling to let this stranger's scrutiny disturb her composure. How dare he look at her in that way? She was a woman grown, and he was making her feel like a chit just out of the schoolroom. She felt confused. And so warm she longed for a fan so she might cool her heated face and neck.

Gregory was speaking, telling her something about Madame Blanchard, the celebrated aeronautist whose balloon had caught fire at a festival in Paris the month before. Thea said everything that was proper regarding the unfortunate lady, but her thoughts were filled with Mr. Colin Jamison, who continued to stare at her.

She had no idea what he thought he was doing, but she wanted him to stop. Now.

Fortunately for Thea's composure, Eloise chose that moment to enter the room. "Thea," she began, "have you seen my—Oh. I beg your pardon. I thought you were alone. I—" She stopped abruptly, apparently only just realizing the identity of the gentlemen who stood at her entrance.

"Eloise," Thea said immediately, afraid her cousin might take it into her head to turn and leave the room as quickly as she had entered it, "how fortunate that you have returned, for we have guests. Mr. Ward you know, of course, but pray allow me to introduce Mr. Jamison."

"Sir," Eloise said, dropping the briefest of curtsies.

"Miss Kendall," the gentleman replied, "it is a pleasure to make your acquaintance at last. Our chance meeting yesterday was far too brief."

Eloise got through the amenities, but all the while her mind raced, searching for some excuse that would allow her to leave the morning room without incurring her cousin's wrath at such rudeness. She had no objection to Mr. Jamison's company, he appeared gentlemanly enough, but she did not wish to remain in the same room with Gregory Ward. He knew it, too. That mocking light in his green eyes told her that he knew she wanted to be any place but here, with him, forced into civility and small talk.

He looked her over slowly, pausing for a millisecond

on her rounded bosom, and making her long to box his ears for the impertinence. "How *very* nice to see you again," he drawled, that detestable crooked smile pulling at the corners of his lips.

The expected reciprocation stuck in Eloise's throat, and had her life depended upon it, she could not have echoed his comment. It was *not* nice to see him again.

"Although," he continued, that mocking light in his eyes evident once again, "I am quite willing to concede that the pleasure is all on my side."

She had drawn breath to tell him that she wanted none of his concessions, when the door burst open again and her young brother rushed in. "Eloise!" Jeremy blurted out. "Cousin Thea! You will never guess what has—Oh."

Like his sister, the lad stopped short at sight of the visitors, but unlike her, his enthusiasm did not abate in the least. Apparently big with news, he had difficulty holding his eagerness in check long enough for the introductions to be made. After bowing politely and shaking hands with each of the gentlemen, he rushed into speech. "Eloise," he began, "I meant to make you guess the nature of my news, but since Mr. Ward is here, I suppose he has already told you about the proposed outing."

"I have not," Gregory said pleasantly, "for I was waiting for the perfect moment to apprise them of the plans." He winked at the boy. "You know how ladies are, they sometimes need to be convinced of the joys in store for them."

Eloise mistrusted the teasing look in Gregory's eyes, and she did not like the conspiratorial smile her brother was trying to hide. "For my part," she said rather haughtily, "I find it quite odious that males invariably feel it is incumbent upon us females to enter into all their likes and interests, no matter how . . . how . . ."

"Odious?" Gregory supplied.

"No matter how *objectionable* those interests might be."

"But, Eloise," Jeremy said, giving her a beseeching look that put her in mind of a poor, starving puppy that has never had a treat in its entire life, "this will not be in the least objectionable. I promise you. Please, please, please do not say we may not go."

"Nor," she continued, as though the lad had not spoken, "are said males the least bit ashamed of wheedling said females, or even demeaning themselves by begging like some pathetic creature."

Apparently not the least bit insulted, her brother mouthed a silent, "Please," after which his sister sighed.

"What is this outing?" she asked. "But be warned, Jeremy Kendall, I make no promises other than that I will listen to the proposal."

The boy smiled broadly, as if it was now a *fait accompli*. "We are to go to Creswell Crags," he announced, as though bestowing upon her a rare treat, "to explore one of the caves."

"What!" both ladies exclaimed at once, their voices filled with a combination of disbelief and loathing.

"Actually," Gregory said, "cave exploration can be a most enjoyable pastime."

"Without a doubt," Eloise said. "Bats. Total darkness. Slime-encrusted walls. Treacherous abysses just waiting for the unwary. *Umm.* What a rare treat."

Gregory laughed. "When we were boys, young Basil's father and uncle, along with my brother and me, spent many happy hours rambling through those caves in search of adventure. I related one or two of those adventures to Basil this past Christmas, and at his insistence, I promised I would take the lad to the Crags when next I came this way."

"Then take him there by all means," Eloise said. "And my brother, too, if that is your wish." She stared at Jeremy, whose shirt and face looked as though they might never come clean. "In fact, should you discover some bottomless chasm, pray cast that disgusting chub into it."

All three of the males laughed, none of them misled by her vehemence. Gregory was the first to speak. "Unfortunately, my uncle refused to let Basil go, even though I told him there was no danger."

"Lord Threwsbury refused his consent? Then surely that is an end to the matter."

"It might have been," Gregory replied, "had I not assured my uncle that cave exploration was so lacking in danger that you ladies would be happy to make a day of it with us."

The ladies most assuredly did *not* wish to make a day of it, nor even a minute of it. Unfortunately, their arguments were not sufficient to convince Gregory Ward that neither of them wished to go to Creswell Crags. Somehow, by the time the gentlemen took their leave of Lady Deighton and her cousins, the expedition was all arranged for the following day.

"Men!" Thea remarked the moment the door closed behind them. "They never play fair."

Eloise nodded in agreement. "Imagine the gall of him, playing on our sympathy by referring to Basil as *a poor, fatherless boy*."

"I see nothing unfair in that," Jeremy said. "After all, I am a poor, fatherless boy myself."

It was as well for the pitiful orphan that he was fast on his feet, for his sister, out of patience with males of all ages, picked up a book and hurled it at her brother's retreating back.

The next day the gentlemen reined in their horses at the dower house promptly at ten of the clock. They were followed moments later by Lord Threwsbury's landau, the tops let down to reveal Basil and his tutor, Mr. Everett Browne. To insure that no harm came to the boy, his lordship had insisted that his own coachman handle the ribbons of the serviceable grays, and sitting beside John Coachman on the raised seat was one of the liveried footmen, his arm resting atop a wicker basket filled to overflowing with food and drink, lest the heir presumptive should be in need of refreshment.

At the same moment the landau arrived, a groom from the Deighton Hall stables appeared around the bend in the carriageway. He led Thea's pretty sorrel mare, as well as the dun-colored mare the new Lord Deighton had designated for Eloise's use, and even before the groom reached the gentlemen, the handsome walnut door to the dower house swung open and Jeremy Kendall came bounding out.

"Good morning," he said, bowing politely to Gregory and Colin, then he climbed aboard the landau. He greeted the young tutor with all due respect, then he acknowledged Basil's presence by yanking the younger boy's cap off his head. With a backhand motion, he sent the cap sailing across the carriageway, toward the banks of the brook, where it landed just short of a bed of brilliant pink phlox.

Naturally, this show of disrespect for the future Lord Threwsbury provoked a bit of good-natured scuffling, but before either boy received more than a shove and a halfhearted punch on the arm, they gave over tussling in favor of a run to the stone footbridge to fetch Basil's cap. After jumping down from the carriage, they raced each other, Jeremy giving the younger and shorter Basil a three-count headstart.

The boys had not yet returned when the ladies appeared. Thea was in especially good looks. She had chosen to wear her new blue habit and the matching jockey bonnet with the snow white osprey feather—a circumstance that left her cousin completely baffled, for like Eloise, Thea had denied any desire whatsoever to accompany the gentlemen to the crags.

Eloise had, of course, chosen to show her dislike of the proposed outing by donning the green faille she had worn many time these past six years. The habit was far from fashionable, and it bore more than a few mud stains around the hem, but to have worn her pretty new claret ensemble would have given the wrong impression. *She,* at least, would be true to her principles.

"How do you do?" she asked Mr. Browne.

"Verrah well, thank you, miss," replied the red-faced young Scotsman, whose burr was always more pronounced when he was in the presence of single females.

Eloise nodded politely to Colin Jamison. "Sir," she said.

"Miss Kendall," replied the gentleman in gray.

Her brief nod to Gregory bordered on rudeness; especially since she spoke not a word to him, but if he noticed the slight, he showed no reaction. Instead, he came forward, his fingers laced together to assist her to mount.

While Mr. Jamison assisted Thea, saying something privately to her that brought a shy smile to her lips, Gregory bent forward so Eloise could put her booted foot in his hands.

When she was ready, he said, "Up you go," then he straightened and tossed her into the saddle as though she weighed no more than she had that time he had pulled her from the pond.

On the pretext of making certain that her foot was safely in the stirrup, he leaned toward her, his words for her ears only. "Since you have obviously decided to give me the cold shoulder, may I hope that you will not eat me alive if I comment upon your attire?"

Thinking he meant to pay her a quite spurious compliment, Eloise was about to tell him to keep his remarks to himself, when he said, "Green is always a good choice for ladies of a certain age."

A certain age! "Why, you insufferable lout! I will have you know that I am just turned four-and-twenty, and I do not consider myself to be—" Eloise bit back the remainder of her diatribe, for she had detected a spark of amusement in his eyes. He was baiting her! "Sir, you are a mannerless boor."

He bowed as if she had paid him a compliment. "And you, madam, could give lessons in rudeness."

Honesty compelled her to acknowledge the truth of his words, though Eloise categorically refused to offer him an apology. "You bring out the worst in me."

"I know," he said softly, "and for that, *I* apologize. Do you suppose there is any chance that we might forget our past differences? Just for today, of course. Just so we do not ruin the day for everyone else."

When she hesitated, he said, "Basil has been looking forward to this outing, and even my uncle's insistence that he bring along his tutor did not dampen the lad's enthusiasm. What do you say? For the sake of the boys, can we call a temporary truce?"

Normally a most agreeable sort, Eloise finally nodded.

"Marvelous," he said, holding his hand out to her. "Have we a pact, then?"

"A temporary truce," Eloise amended, but she placed her gloved hand in his in a sportsmanlike manner.

To her surprise, Gregory did not shake her hand. Instead, he used his forefinger to move aside the soft kid that covered her wrist, then he brushed his lips across her exposed skin. The contact lasted no more than a moment, but the warmth of his touch sent a jolt of awareness all the way to Eloise's midsection.

"Who knows," he said softly, still holding her hand, "if you got to know me, you might like me."

Still shaken by her reaction to his touch, Eloise snatched her hand away. "If I were you, I would not wager money on that possibility."

The ride to Creswell Crag required just under two hours to complete, including the one brief stop they made near a tributary of the Derwent River, where everyone stretched their limbs and enjoyed a drink of the cool, clear water. The hilly grassland on either side of the river had been lush and green, but as the party traveled the final few miles, the terrain became gradually steeper and less idyllic. The trees grew more sparsely, and in the distance Eloise saw the gray cliffs of the narrow gorge known as the Crags.

To her surprise, she found herself feeling more excited the nearer they got to their destination. Not that she would have admitted that fact to anyone. Still, she had heard a bit of Mr. Browne's impromptu lecture on the significance of the Crags to the geologists who studied the gorge and the paleo scientists who came to view the limestone caves, and Eloise was eager to see the place that had once been home to prehistoric cave dwellers.

When they finally arrived at their destination, which was a relatively flat meadow where the horses could graze, the adventurers left the animals in the capable hands of the two male servants, then began the final portion of their journey on foot. Since they were all in agreement that Gregory should be their guide, they followed him without question when he began the slow, somewhat arduous walk up the rough foot path that gave access to the closest, as well as the largest, of the caves.

They were on the western side of the Crags, but as they walked, it was possible to look across the gorge and see the eastern cliff face, where dozens of cave entrances were visible. After looking their fill of the gray sandstone that appeared to stretch for miles to the north and to the south, they spared a few minutes to look down into the deep, frighteningly beautiful gorge, with its stunted trees and jagged outcroppings.

"About a fortnight ago," Jeremy announced, "a dog fell over the side quite near here."

Upon hearing this interesting tidbit, Eloise backed away a pace or two, never very comfortable with heights. "Poor dog," she said.

"Do not be concerned, ma'am," Mr. Browne said, "for the animal came to no harm. According to the article in the paper, some climbers found him four days later, lying on a shallow ledge, hungry and thirsty, but otherwise none the worse for the experience."

Not at all reassured, Eloise held her breath when Jeremy and Basil insisted on lying on their stomachs to hang their heads over the edge of the precipice. They were spitting, to see how far down the canyon wall the spittle would fall, when Eloise recalled that just the day before Basil had gotten a bit too close to the edge of the bank of the weir and had fallen head-first into the water.

That did it! Two falls were more than she could contemplate without shuddering, and she wanted the boys out of harm's way. Knowing how her brother disliked being *coddled,* as he called it, in front of others, Eloise called to him, feigning a rather bored attitude. "Boys," she said, "come away, do. Unless, of course, you fancy becoming food for those hawks I see soaring in the distance."

"Aw, Eloise. The hawks did not eat the dog."

Not at all reassured, she said, "You might not be as fortunate as the dog. The bottom of the gorge is a long way down, and if you two should tumble over the side, you might be obliged to remain there indefinitely. With the possible exception of Mr. Ward, who is an experienced climber, not one of us could climb down to retrieve your battered and broken bodies."

Naturally, the lads found this rather gory picture quite to their liking, but after a moment they left the edge and rejoined the adults on the narrow, pebble-strewn path.

Gregory took the lead once again, and Thea and Colin Jamison brought up the rear. Mr. Jamison had offered Thea his arm, which she had taken gratefully, and as the path steepened, the two of them lagged farther and farther behind. Eloise had politely declined Mr. Browne's offer of assistance, bidding the embarrassed young man conserve his energy so he could keep an eye on the two boys, who seemed to be growing more excited with each step that brought them closer to the cave.

As for Gregory, who was not even breathing hard, he remained unusually quiet. After one long, unreadable look at Eloise when she had called to the boys to come away from the precipice, he had merely thrown over his shoulder the rather unwieldy looking wooden-framed knapsack he had taken from the floor of the landau; then he had turned and continued to lead the way.

Once they finally reached the mouth of the cave, the purpose of the knapsack became apparent, for Gregory laid it on the ground, unbuttoned the flap, and removed the contents. First came a pair of tallow candles, then a pouch made of waxed cloth to make it water repellent; next he removed a pair of oddly shaped lanterns, whose side and back panels were silvered to multiply the light and direct it straight ahead.

The pouch contained wooden splinters that had been coated with chlorate of potash, and a small vial of oil of vitriol. Gregory chose one of the splinters, then while he dipped it into the small vial, Eloise held her breath, aware that if he spilled the oil of vitriol on his skin, it would cause a painful burn. She need not have worried, for Gregory had obviously done this before. He needed only one try to produce the necessary burst of fire, which he used to light the candle wicks.

Cupping his hand around the wicks to shield the flames, he placed first one candle then the other in a well inside the respective lanterns. When the candles were secure, he closed the glass doors of the lanterns to protect the flames against any sudden puffs of air.

"Mr. Browne," he said, passing one of the lanterns to the tutor, "if you will be so good as to bring up the rear, I will lead the way, with everyone else staying between us. That way, there should be sufficient light for even the most . . . shall we say, *reluctant* explorer."

Eloise knew he referred to her, but she was far too

pleased to see the lanterns to protest his amusement at her expense.

"As for the bats," he said, looking directly at the two boys, "unless you do something to disturb them—which I strongly recommend you not even consider doing—they will, in all likelihood, remain close to the ceiling, where they are happiest."

In the space of a heartbeat he murmured rather close to Eloise's ear, "If, perchance, one of those little flying mammals should come near you, Miss Kendall, please feel free to tuck your face against my chest."

She wanted to tell him in no-uncertain terms what she thought of his suggestion, but a persistent little qualm cautioned her not to spurn the offer out of hand. She might live to regret it.

As it turned out, Eloise had ventured scarcely twenty feet into the tunnel leading to the cave before she knew it would take more than the threat of bats to turn her back. This was adventure indeed, and she meant to see it through to the end!

Thea, on the other hand, discovered within herself a hitherto unknown aversion to being in closed spaces, and after only a minute, she apologized, but stated that she really could not remain. "I . . . I know I am behaving badly, but I feel as if the walls are closing in on me. Forgive me, but I really must go back out into the air. Immediately!"

No one witnessing the trembling of her lips or the rapid movement of her chest as she attempted to draw breath into her lungs could doubt the sincerity of her fear. Mr. Jamison was the first to react. "Come, ma'am," he said, "I have seen all I care to see." Without another word, he put his arm around Thea's shoulders and led her back out into the sunshine.

When Eloise turned to follow them, Gregory caught

her by the wrist, detaining her. "Do you wish to leave?" he asked.

She shook her head. "Not at all. I should like to stay."

"Then do so. I promise you, I will let nothing happen to you."

"But what of Thea? She may have need of me."

"You may trust Colin to do all that is necessary to insure your cousin's comfort."

Eloise hesitated only a moment, then she nodded.

"Good girl. Now," he said loud enough for the boys and Mr. Browne to hear, "what say you we begin our exploration of the past."

The boys cheered, causing a surprisingly loud echo that was answered by a prolonged series of squeals from the numerous winged inhabitants of the cave. When the frenzy finally subsided, and the bat population returned once again to the peace of the ceiling, Mr. Browne cautioned his pupils to remember Mr. Ward's admonition and not to behave recklessly.

Reckless or not, Eloise had never thought to experience such excitement. To begin with, the ceiling of the tunnel was high enough to permit even Gregory to walk upright, and it was wide enough so that no one needed to touch the walls. As for the tunnel floor, the earth was surprisingly smooth, with no holes or hidden roots to trip the unwary.

"The smoothness," Gregory told her, as if reading her mind, "is the result of hundreds, perhaps thousands of feet treading in and out of this cave entrance for who knows how many generations."

"Very true," Mr. Browne added. "The inhabitants of these limestone caves—people whose tools were made entirely of stone—were the oldest known people of Europe. Perhaps of the entire world. And scientists can only guess at how long, or how long ago, these people may have dwelled here in the Crags."

"Eons and eons?" Jeremy asked, his voice hushed with wonder.

"As to that," his tutor replied, "no one can say. At least, not with any degree of accuracy. I doubt that we will ever know the time period for certain, for there is no way to measure something like that. One might as well ask how old is a rock? It is enough, I believe, that the cave dwellers were here, and that we have evidence of their lives."

Eloise felt a shiver run up her spine, just knowing that her feet were following the same path taken by people who lived so very long ago. However long ago that might have been. "Only think, Jeremy. These people could not have been so unlike us. They would need water and food, and I imagine that many a boy your age, and Basil's age, must have run back and forth through this tunnel, bringing in water and perhaps nuts and berries."

"Actually," Gregory said, "I am persuaded theirs was a male-dominated society. The men were mighty hunters, so I imagine they left the gathering of water and berries to the women."

All Eloise's newly found tolerance of Gregory Ward evaporated. "And just how could you possibly know that? Perhaps it was the women who were the mighty hunters."

Not the least bit offended by her dispute of his assertion, Gregory said, "I merely report what I deduced from the testimony of the cave-dwellers themselves."

Only slightly mollified, she said, "What testimony?"

"Come, see for yourself."

Gregory took her hand, and though she stiffened for a moment, making him suspect that she would like nothing better than to pull away from him, she allowed him to lead her into the cave itself. As he suspected, her first view of the enormous room was followed by a gasp.

"Oh, my," she said, the words coming from her on a rush of exhaled air. "It . . . it is unbelievable."

"Zounds!" Jeremy said, stopping just behind his sister.

"Jupiter!" Basil added in agreement, his mouth falling open in astonishment.

"Well, now," Mr. Browne said, every bit as amazed as his students, "this is something like!"

Gregory had known they would be astounded, for he had never forgotten the first time he and his older brother had stepped inside the large cave. They had been speechless with awe, for the place was one immense, cavernous room, with the roof so high above their heads that the lantern light could not reach far enough to illuminate it.

"Notice the circular depression in the very center of the room," he said.

They all looked where he pointed, to a circle that was dug at least a foot deep. It covered fully half the available floor space and was rimmed with hundreds of stones, fist-sized and larger. Around the outside of the major circle, at more or less regular intervals, were two or three dozen smaller circles, each one rimmed by stones.

"I always imagined," Gregory said, his voice hushed, yet eerily resonant in the huge chamber, "that the inner circle was the common meeting ground for ceremonies and the like, while the smaller circles might have contained the fires of the different family groups."

"It sounds reasonable," Eloise said. "There can be

no doubt that the circles were planned. As for the rocks, they are the same gray limestone found on the floor of the gorge, so someone must have brought them in here on purpose."

"By Jove," Mr. Browne said. "Looking at this lot, one would have to suppose that the people who lived here had a more organized culture than one would have suspected." He held his lantern aloft, so that the light shone on the nearest section of wall. "Oh! By Jove!" he said again, the excitement obvious in his voice, "will ye look at that."

The young Scotsman did not need to invite the other three to give their attention to the walls, for they were already staring, apparently rendered speechless by what they saw.

Gregory understood their astonishment, for he had felt much the same the first time he had discovered the carvings on the walls.

On this section of the wall was depicted a hunting scene in which at least a dozen men took part. Each man carried a long, sticklike weapon with a pointed stone lashed to the end, and the beast they surrounded was shown as being at least twice as tall and three times as broad as the men who hunted it.

"Is it a dinosaur?" Jeremy asked, his voice quiet, almost reverent.

"Perhaps," Gregory replied. "I could never tell for certain. My brother maintained that it was some sort of bison, but I would never agree to its being a grass-eating bovine, even a prehistoric one. I much preferred to think of it as some fierce flesh-eater, one who might at any moment swoop down upon the hunters and devour one or two of them."

Both Jeremy and Basil were in complete agreement with Gregory's interpretation of the carving, and though Eloise was inclined to agree with the gentleman's brother's somewhat more prosaic version, she kept her opinion to herself. She saw no reason to spoil the drama for the boys.

The fascinated adventurers circled the entire room, shining their lantern light on every inch of the cave walls. They found seventeen scenes in all—some carved better than others—and each scene depicted yet another hunting party overpowering some mammoth prey.

Just before they arrived back at their starting point, Gregory called Eloise's attention to a small section of wall. "Look there," he said.

He shone the lantern light directly on an especially fine carving, without doubt the finest in the cave. In this scene, several females of varying size sat in a circle, using a round stone to grind something that lay in the bottom of a stone bowl. "Women's work," he said, "in more ways than one."

Eloise was too captivated by what she saw to return to their dispute over whether this cave society was, or was not, male-dominated. It was enough for her that she had been allowed to see this marvelous record of a society so long gone from this earth.

She was still lost in the wonder of the final carving, when Basil spied something imbedded in the wall, down low, near the ground. "Shine the light over here, please, Cousin Gregory, for I have found an insect of some sort."

The men turned both the lights on Basil's discovery, and everyone bent close to have a look. What the boy had found was an insect right enough, and though Eloise was no expert on bugs, she felt certain she had never seen anything quite like that creature. A shelled insect about the size of a shilling, it was black, and its body was divided into three sections, with the middle section possessed of dozens of legs.

Mr. Browne explained that the creature had been trapped in a resinous goo that had later solidified, thereby preserving the insect for who knew how long.

After everyone had *oohed* and *ahhed* over that particular wonder, Basil asked his cousin if he had brought his pocket knife.

"As always," Gregory replied. "Have you need of it?"

"Yes, sir. The insect is quite near the surface, and I should like to dig him out and take him home with me. He would make a marvelous watch fob."

"Take nothing with you," Gregory said, and though he spoke softly, the tone of his voice brooked no argument. "Just because you found something, it does not automatically follow that what you found is yours. Everything in this cave belongs to history, and to all those people who will come here in the future. People like us, who will be surprised at what they find, and awed that it has lain here undisturbed for countless centuries."

"Y—yes, sir," the boy stammered. "You are right, of course. I did not think."

"Of course you did not. That is why I ventured to give you a bit of a hint."

Later, when the entire party had returned to the landau and the waiting alfresco nuncheon, Jeremy told his sister in private, "If that was a 'hint,' I should not like to hear a full-blown speech."

Eloise shared a laugh with her brother, but if she had been honest, she would have admitted that she quite agreed with Gregory's reading of the situation. He had shown real sensitivity to the need for respecting historical finds—a subject that was rather close to

Eloise's heart. Like a number of other British subjects, Eloise had been incensed on behalf of the citizens of Greece, when Lord Elgin removed the celebrated Grecian marbles from their rightful place and brought them to London for society to admire.

Momentarily in sympathy with her longtime nemesis, Eloise unbent so far as to allow Gregory to employ his pocket knife to peel for her one of the plump, pink peaches grown in his uncle's orangery.

"For you," he said moments later, presenting the fruit to her, cut into bite-sized slices.

"Thank you," she said. "It looks delicious."

Eloise had just put a piece of the luscious fruit into her mouth when the temporary truce between her and Gregory Ward came to an abrupt end. In a matter of seconds, the infuriating man set her back up once again, nearly causing her to choke.

"Ma'am," he said to Thea, "I believe someone told me that you have planned a musicale for tomorrow evening."

"Yes," Thea replied, "I have. It is to be our first entertainment since we removed to the dower house."

"If it would not crowd your rooms too much," he said in front of everyone, so she could not possibly refuse him without appearing unconscionably rude, "would you be so kind as to allow Mr. Jamison and me to attend your party?"

Chapter Four

"Thea! How could you?"

Her cousin found it unnecessary to ask what Eloise meant by the question. "Pray, what would you have had me do?"

They had entered the dower house only moments before, and Eloise had followed her cousin up the carpeted stairs and into that lady's pretty lilac and silver bedchamber. "You could have told him there was not room enough."

"No, I could not. Due to the unexpectedness of the question, I could not think of a single reason why they could not join us."

"A circumstance Gregory Ward knew full well!"

"What if he did? You know as well as I do that the guest list is made up of people we see year in and year out. Personally, I do not find it so contemptible to spice up the musicale by including two unquestionably fashionable and sophisticated London gentlemen."

"A sly fox, more like. Why, Gregory Ward has no more manners than a wild beast."

"Coming it a bit strong, Eloise. Both men are quite *top of the trees,* I believe the saying is. And even if they were less so, I should still feel honored that they wished to attend our little soiree."

"But—"

"If memory serves," Thea interrupted, "you told me

just the other day that I was entitled to attend a few more entertainments before donning caps and sitting with the chaperons. I presume you were being sincere. You did mean it, did you not?"

"Of course I meant it. You are much too young and lovely to be thinking of yourself as being past the age for enjoying a bit of fun."

Though Thea's face grew pink at the compliment, she said, "Well, then?"

Hoist by her own petard, Eloise muttered something beneath her breath, then she turned and exited the bedchamber.

When Thea was finally alone, she crossed the soft carpet with its pattern of silver leaves and stopped at the window that overlooked the brook and the small stone footbridge. Always charmed by the view, she gazed at it for a time, hoping the peaceful scene might quiet her disordered thoughts. It did not.

The day had proved more disconcerting than she could ever have imagined. From the moment she had finished her morning toast and chocolate, then decided to wear her new azure habit, Thea knew she was not herself. She was well aware that Eloise expected her to wear something old, as a protest against their having been coerced into riding to Creswell Crags, but when Thea had recalled the gentleman in gray, with his black, staring eyes, she had donned the azure.

Then, of course, while Colin Jamison had assisted her into the saddle, he had whispered very close to her ear, sending long-forgotten sensations up Thea's spine, and making a jumble of her usually well-ordered thoughts.

"You are lovely," he had said very softly. "Quite the most beautiful woman I have ever seen."

Thea felt certain it could not be true. After all, he

was an important man—one who moved in the first circles of politics and society—and he was so handsome Thea felt weak just looking at his face. Surely he must claim acquaintance with hundreds of beautiful women. Still, the softly spoken words had made her feel all warm inside—warm and desirable—and more alive than she had been in a very long time.

For the two hours needed to complete their journey, Thea had kept reminding herself not to make more of a simple compliment than it deserved. And yet, when they arrived at the Crags, and Colin Jamison had lifted her down from the mare's saddle, Thea's heart had begun to race like a startled hare.

Mr. Jamison had offered her his arm for the walk up the rough footpath, but that meant nothing; any gentleman would have done the same. The shy Mr. Browne made a similar offer to Eloise.

It was later that Thea began to think she was not imagining things, and that something was happening between her and the gentleman from London.

They had ventured only a few feet into the cave entrance, with everyone excited about the novelty of exploring beneath the ground, when Thea began to regret coming into the musty darkness, and she feared she might embarrass herself at any moment by screaming like some deranged woman.

She was too frightened to continue, yet too frightened to turn and leave. She had reached the limit of her endurance when Colin Jamison came close and placed a protective arm around her shoulders.

"Come," he said quietly, then he led her back out into the sunshine.

He had found a likely boulder, then spread his clean linen handkerchief over it so she might sit down without ruining her skirt. When she was seated, he kneeled beside her, holding her hands until she ceased to tremble. It was then that Thea knew he was not merely flirting with her. Whatever the dark-eyed gentleman had in mind—and Thea could not, would not, even hazard a guess as to what that might be—he was in earnest.

Now, as she gazed at the brook and the stone footbridge her husband had built some years ago, Thea warned herself not to let what happened today beguile her into imagining things and events that might never come to pass. That way lay heartbreak.

For the moment, it was enough to know that she would be in the gentleman's company once again, at tomorrow evening's musicale.

Unlike her cousin, Thea had not been displeased that Gregory Ward had made his request in front of the others. Good manners decreed that she not refuse him, not with so many people privy to her every word; so, of course, she had not done so. It would remain Thea's secret that she had not wished to refuse him.

Later that day, when Colin and Gregory met in the billiards room at Threwsbury Park, Gregory could not hide his smile. "By my reckoning, Colin old boy, you owe me a favor."

"Oh?" replied the dark-haired gentleman. "And why is that?"

"Do not play the fool, sir, for you know to what I refer. The musicale. I count it a stroke of genius that I happened to see my uncle's invitation on his desk, for now you will have a perfectly legitimate excuse for being in Lady Deighton's company for the evening. Thea sings like a bird, and should someone suggest a duet, you might discover an occasion to join your voice with hers."

"If I am asked, I shall, of course, be most happy to sing."

"Select a romantic duet," Gregory suggested, "and you might be forgiven for holding her hands, or even slipping an arm around her waist."

Mr. Jamison gave him a measuring look; then, apparently feeling it would be fruitless to attempt to deny his interest in Theadosia Deighton, he smiled. "I admit nothing, sir. As for my owing you a favor, I say only that you may rest assured that I always honor my debts."

Gregory let the matter rest, not wanting to force confidences his friend might not wish to share. Instead, he removed his coat and laid it across the back of a chair. When he turned around, however, he noticed that the party whip was studying him, a speculative look in his eyes.

"I do not trust that look," Gregory said, "and I have been acquainted with you long enough now to realize that when you touch your finger to your mustache, it is a certain sign that you are mulling something over."

Colin picked up the chalk cube and coated the end of his billiard cue. "I was thinking about your future in politics."

"*My* future? If that is the case, may I know the gist of those thoughts?"

When Colin hesitated, Gregory bid him not turn shy at this late date. "Go ahead, out with it. Though something warns me that I will not like what I hear."

Colin smiled. "I was thinking how the right sort of wife is of untold benefit to a man with political ambitions."

"And you were thinking this on *my* behalf?"

"Definitely on your behalf. It is you, after all, who is seeking election."

"Yes, but—"

"You must know that the voters believe a married man to be more stable, more likely to understand their problems."

"I do know it, just as you must know that none of the ladies of my acquaintance would be considered suitable."

Colin touched his mustache again. "There is Miss Kendall."

"Impossible! I beg of you, Colin, do not go down that road, for Eloise Kendall and I are like oil and water. We simply do not mix."

Though Eloise was not privy to the conversation between the two political gentlemen, she voiced very much the same sentiments the next morning when she sat in the ostentatiously furnished drawing room of Mrs. Parker-Smith. Eloise had come prepared to offer the mean-spirited battle-ax her sincerest apologies for having missed tea on Monday—to grovel if necessary—anything to secure a contribution for the schoolbooks.

As it turned out, the thin, middle-aged matron waved aside the apology, for she was much more interested in discussing the two gentlemen she had seen driving through the village that very Monday. "They were in a smart phaeton," she said, "drawn by a pair of costly looking chestnuts, and I could not help but notice that both the driver and the gentleman who sat beside him were quite handsome."

Recognizing the spark of interest in the woman's hawkish eyes, Eloise furnished her with the information she sought. "The driver was Lord Threwsbury's nephew, Mr. Gregory Ward. His traveling companion was Mr. Colin Jamison."

Mrs. Parker-Smith smiled, if one could call the stretching of those thin lips a smile. Whatever the gesture was called, the sentiment behind it was as spurious as it was calculating, and Eloise warned herself to be on guard.

"I have it on good authority, Miss Kendall, that you and Lady Deighton were seen riding with those same gentleman just yesterday."

Nosy old biddy!

"Yes, ma'am. A party was got up to take my brother and the earl's grandson to Creswell Crags, so they might explore the caves."

"How delightful," her hostess said. After placing her teacup on the Pembroke table beside her chair, she leaned forward, as if to convey the impression of willing confidante. "I was informed, Miss Kendall, that the earl's nephew rode at your side. Am I to wish you and Mr. Ward happy?"

Eloise was aghast. "Gregory Ward and me? My dear madam, you might just as well attempt to mix oil and water. Believe me, the gentleman and I do not even like one another. We never have."

"You don't say so?"

Mrs. Parker-Smith sat back in her chair, quite pleased with what she had heard, and Eloise, not at all reluctant to make use of the woman's mellow mood, broached the subject of the contribution. "As you know, ma'am, we—Reverend Underwood and I—are in dire need of money to purchase schoolbooks. If you could see your way—"

"I understand that Mr. Ward is unwed. Is he engaged, do you know?"

To keep from screaming, Eloise chose a macaroon

from the tea tray and stuffed the sweet into her mouth. She did not wish to discuss Gregory Ward. She had come here to further the cause of the village school, not the ambitions of this social-climbing harridan.

Her hostess tapped a bony finger against the front of her small, pointy teeth, obviously impatient for a reply to her question.

After hastily chewing and swallowing the cookie, Eloise said, "I believe the gentleman is still heart-free."

Heart-less, more like!

Mrs. Parker-Smith nodded as if the information received merely confirmed what she already knew. "Heart-free," she repeated. "How perfectly delightful."

The woman paused, then after a few moments of silence, she gave Eloise a look worthy of an eagle eyeing a plump rabbit. "If only there was some way I could introduce my sweet little girl to the gentleman's notice."

Eloise had bitten into another macaroon, and she almost choked. Gregory Ward and Sylvia Parker-Smith! Impossible!

Gregory, with his broad back and his noticeably muscular physique, was well over six feet tall, while Sylvia, who had only just turned seventeen, was as thin as a rail, and measured no more than four feet ten. The idea of a match between those two completely dissimilar creatures was ludicrous. They might almost have been of different species.

Naturally, Eloise did not give voice to that opinion. While she was lost in picturing Gregory Ward, with his assertive manners, paired with a female who was so timid she would not say boo to a goose, the girl's mother had continued to speak.

"We need only the opportunity," she said, "and someone willing to introduce us. After that, I shall know what to do. The courtship can be left entirely in my hands."

Courtship! The woman certainly did not let moss grow beneath her feet.

After a moment, Eloise realized that Mrs. Parker-Smith was staring at her in a calculating manner. "If there was some way, Miss Kendall, that you could help us in this matter of the introduction—you who are on intimate terms with Lord Threwsbury and his family—I would be most appreciative. In fact, I am persuaded that Mr. Parker-Smith and I could see our way to funding those schoolbooks you mentioned."

Eloise could not believe her ears. She was actually being offered a bribe—she could call it nothing else—to introduce Gregory Ward to Sylvia Parker-Smith. When she made no reply, her hostess continued.

"What say you, Miss Kendall? Would two hundred pounds cover the nonsense?"

Two hundred! Eloise's breath caught in her throat. She had hoped for fifty pounds . . . seventy-five at the most. With two hundred she could buy the needed books, hire a second schoolmaster instead of only the one, and have enough money left over to see to the rethatching of the unused cottage the vicar had persuaded Sir Boris Pilcher to allow them to occupy free of charge for the first year.

And all Eloise had to do to receive this most welcome windfall was introduce Gregory Ward to the Parker-Smiths.

"Ma'am, I—"

"A moment," her hostess said. She excused herself

and left the drawing room. When she returned, she laid a roll of ten-pound notes on the table beside the tea tray. She said nothing more, but let the money speak for itself.

Eloise stared at the roll of soft, as her brother called it, for what seemed a long time, debating with herself over the ethics of accepting a contribution with conditions attached. Finally, after taking a deep, steadying breath, she said, "I wonder, ma'am, do you and Miss Parker-Smith mean to attend my cousin's party this evening?"

"Unfortunately, we were promised to the Wexhams, in Cromford, for a card party. We had already accepted when dear Lady Deighton's card of invitation arrived for the musicale." Another of those thin-lipped smiles appeared. "Ought I to send Mrs. Wexham a note of regret, do you think?"

Eloise reached over and picked up the money, then she removed the napkin from her lap and stood. "You should most definitely not miss this evening's musicale, ma'am. Lord Threwsbury's guests are among those who have promised to be there, and I am persuaded both gentlemen would be pleased to make the acquaintance of some of the citizens of Mansfield Downs."

Once Eloise heard the Parker-Smiths' butler close the door behind her, she walked rather quickly down the short carriageway. "Fleeing the scene of the crime," she muttered.

Not that she felt the least bit of shame for having taken Mrs. Parker-Smith's bribe. To the contrary. Though quite certain her lack of remorse indicated an equal lack of character, Eloise brushed the thought aside, convinced that the needs of the village children took precedence over any qualms she might have about acting as a paid matchmaker.

Politicians accepted money all the time from people who wanted some particular favor in return. Could it be so bad? For all Eloise knew, the sole reason Gregory and Mr. Jamison wished to attend the musicale was to mingle with the guests—mingle and solicit political contributions. She could think of no other reason for them wanting to be there.

Furthermore, who was to say that the odious Gregory Ward and the insipid Sylvia Parker-Smith would not suit one another to a nicety?

Chapter Five

Gregory was normally an early riser. His energy level was high, and it would not allow him to lie abed overlong. On the morning following the trip to Creswell Crags, he was up well before the other inhabitants of the house, and after making a quick raid of the kitchen for a thick slab of bread with butter, he took a shortcut through the herb garden then continued on his way to the stables.

Ten minutes later, he was astride the large, dark bay gelding he had ridden yesterday. Horse and man traveled at a clipping pace down the carriageway of Threwsbury Park, both happy to be out in the fresh morning air, with nothing more serious on their minds than a good, fast run.

Gregory had been coming to his uncle's estate for as long as he could remember, so he was well acquainted with the best routes to take. Since he meant to eschew the lane and ride across country, he knew he would need to make a sharp left just beyond the wrought-iron entrance gates. His objective was a dip in the low stone wall, where the horse could jump without risk of injury, yet gain immediate access to the open fields just on the other side of the lane.

First, though, he must pass the deserted brick gatehouse, where at least a dozen thick, fragrant yews flanked the once handsome building. When Gregory was a child, the two-room gatehouse had been occupied by an eccentric cousin of his lordship's, and the yews had been meticulously pruned into urnlike shapes. In the past dozen years, however, the gatehouse had been unoccupied and the shrubs had been left to nature's devices, until they had grown into fortresslike displays.

As horse and rider hurried toward the gates, Gregory thought he saw someone—or some thing—dart behind the yews to the right. Unsure what he had seen, but quite certain that it would be reckless beyond permission to turn and look back over his shoulder while the gelding galloped at full speed, Gregory continued on his way.

"Probably just a deer," he muttered into the wind that whipped about his face.

Lord Threwsbury had given up hunting a number of years ago, and as a result, the population of red deer at the Park had increased steadily. Not that Gregory begrudged the animals the run of the place. They were beautiful creatures, shy and unthreatening, and as far as he was concerned there was room enough at the Park for both man and beast.

As for *him* thinning out the herd, as his uncle had suggested on more than one occasion, Gregory had flatly refused the invitation. To him, aiming a loaded gun at an unarmed and thoroughly peaceful animal was not true sport. Let the deer eat their fill of the gatehouse yews, the shrubs would come to no harm from a bit of pruning.

Having put the incident from his mind, Gregory rode on, giving himself up to the joy of the ride and the beauty of the hilly grasslands of the downs.

As it happened, Gregory was not the only one of Lord Threwsbury's guests who bestirred himself that morning. Colin Jamison was no more a slug-abed than his friend, but he kept that fact to himself. He had no wish for company. Every morning—in fair weather or foul—he enjoyed a solitary walk in Green Park, which was opposite his rooms in London. The members of the *ton* never ventured out before noon, so the party whip was guaranteed a private commune with nature—a moment of solitude before taking up the serious business of politics.

That particular morning, the gentleman in gray chose to exit the house by way of the French windows in Lord Threwsbury's library, his purpose to stroll a bit across the rear of the parkland. Unlike the prospect from the front of the house, the land to the rear had been left as nature had made it, gloriously "unimproved" by the gardeners' scythes.

The day was crisp and clear, with a sky so blue a man could believe it truly reached to heaven, and to Colin, the freshness of the air was more invigorating than a tonic.

He had walked for quite some time, and though it was not a part of his plan to venture onto the Deighton property, he soon found himself on a slight hill that offered an unimpaired view of the dower house and a small wildflower garden to the rear. Someone moved about in the garden—a lady with a shallow basket over her arm—and though Colin was not close enough to see her face, he knew without question that the lady was Thea.

Even when employed in so mundane a task as cutting flowers, she was grace itself. Colin watched her for several minutes, content to admire the elegance of her posture, the charm of the slender figure beneath the simple sprigged muslin. He might have remained undetected, had an excited little terrier not come run-

ning toward him, barking its high-pitched warning to
cease and desist.

"Angus!" Thea called. "What is it? What mischief
are you up to now, you silly—" She paused, words
failing her, for the dog had discovered a man. A slender gentleman dressed in gray. It was Mr. Jamison,
Thea knew that the instant she saw him standing there
on the hill.

But what was he doing there? And how long had
he been doing it?

"Sir?" she called. "Is that you, Mr. Jamison?"

The gentleman tipped his hat and made as if to
come toward her, but the terrier would not let him
pass. The little black-and-white dog stood his ground,
growling as if he meant to guard every inch of the
estate—guard it with his life if necessary.

"Angus," Thea called again, "come here, boy."

When the terrier did not obey her, but continued
his *yip, yip, yip* until Thea thought the din would damage her ears, she set her basket and scissors on the
ground, lifted the hem of her skirt, then hurried up
the hill toward the supposed malefactor and the excited little dog.

"How do you do?" Mr. Jamison said. "I did not
mean to interrupt, ma'am, and I would have passed
on by without a word had your attack dog not seen
fit to announce my presence. A terrier, is he?"

"More like a holy terror," she said, reaching down
and scooping the animal up into her arms. "Angus
belongs to Perdita, the new Lady Deighton, but I am
afraid the silly creature feels obliged to protect the
entire estate."

Realizing what she had said, Thea chuckled. "By
'silly creature' I meant the dog, of course, not Lady
Deighton."

Mr. Jamison laughed as well. "You put my mind at ease, ma'am, for I was feeling quite unnerved, thinking the new Lady Deighton might come charging toward me at any moment, weapon drawn and ready for use."

Mr. Jamison reached out his hand and let the dog sniff at him. "You are a marvelous fellow, Angus old boy, and you did your job with commendable speed and diligence. However, there is no need to eat me, I assure you."

Apparently having decided to reverse his previous assessment of the stranger, Angus stopped barking, wagged his tail in welcome, and began licking Mr. Jamison's hand as if in slavish devotion.

"Some watchdog you are," Thea scolded. "Only let a man pay you a compliment, and you turn toady on the instant."

Thea bent to set the little dog on the ground, and when she straightened, Mr. Jamison was regarding her in that way he had, as though she were the most interesting person he had ever met.

Feeling unaccountably breathless, Thea said, "May I offer you a cup of tea?"

"You are very kind, ma'am. I should love a cup."

At his smile, a wave of warmth swept over Thea, and while they walked down the hill toward the little wildflower garden, it occurred to her that she was little better than Angus. One smile from Colin Jamison and she was acting like the veriest simpleton.

When they reached the house, Thea stepped inside the kitchen and asked Cook if they might have tea brought to them in the garden, then while they waited, she bid Mr. Jamison be seated on one of the little wrought-iron chairs beside a bed of tall, cherry red prince's feathers.

"I see you were cutting flowers, ma'am. Pray, do

not let me stop you from finishing your task. Are the blossoms in the basket meant to make up arrangements for the musicale?"

She nodded. "Perdita very kindly invited me to take what I would from the rose garden at the main house, but I declined the offer. Tending that garden was a particular joy of my husband's, and now that he is gone, I find it painful to go there For that reason," she added, "my guests will have to make do with vases of dahlias, cyclamen, and delphinium,"

"I have no doubt the guests will be enchanted." After a moment, he said, "Yours was a love match?"

In anyone else, Thea would have considered the question unforgivably personal, but something in Colin Jamison's face bid her not take offense.

"Perhaps not at first," she said, "but no one could be in John's presence for long without coming to care for him. He was the kindest man I have ever known."

The awkward moment that followed was interrupted by the maid, who came outside bearing a tray containing a pewter teapot, two translucent china cups and saucers, and a plate of steaming currant buns.

"Now that," her guest said, his voice filled with enthusiasm, "is a most welcome sight, for I am quite famished."

Thea was grateful to him for his sensitivity in not asking further questions about her husband, and she poured him a cup of tea and passed it to him straight away.

After a surprisingly companionable silence, in which the gentleman devoured two of the delicious buns and allowed his cup to be refilled twice, he wiped his sticky fingers on his napkin, set the linen on the little wrought-iron table, then said he must be going.

"While I am thinking of it, ma'am, I have it on good authority that you have a glorious singing voice, and I wondered if you were familiar with *Don Giovanni*?"

"Mozart's opera? Of course."

"And the duet between Zerlina and Giovanni? Do you know it?"

"Why, yes. I know it well. Why do you ask?"

Mr. Jamison glanced away for just a moment, and when he looked back at her once again, Thea detected just the tiniest hint of diffidence in his smile.

What was this? The powerful party whip shy?

The man had a chink in his armor, and Thea would not have believed it if she had not seen it with her own eyes. And yet, for some reason she did not wish to analyze too closely, she found the touch of vulnerability surprisingly endearing.

"I wondered, ma'am, if you would do me the honor of allowing me to join you in the duet?"

"Join me?" Thea repeated, all but choking on her own breath. "In a duet?"

"If you please," he said.

At the softly spoken words, a familiar warmth slowly winded its way through Thea's body, arousing a yearning she had thought buried with her husband. What on earth was wrong with her? Colin Jamison had suggested they sing a duet, and she was reacting as though he had asked her to come away with him to a deserted island, where they would lie beneath the stars and make passionate love to one another.

"I . . . I should like that very much," she said.

Later, after she had watched Colin Jamison climb the hill and disappear from view, Thea was obliged to remind herself that it was the shared song she had meant she would like very much.

*   *   *

Because Gregory had been deprived of real exercise since leaving his home three days ago, he rode for longer than he had intended, without giving much thought to where he wandered.

When the open fields gave way to a small wood just to the west of the village, he slowed the gelding to a trot, lest they run afoul of some low-hanging tree branch. On one such branch, hidden within the green leaves of a turkey oak tree, a turtledove cooed to his mate, while closer to the ground, songbirds flitted around the laden branches of a mulberry bush, feasting on the green, yellow, and gold fruit that had only just begun to ripen.

After a time, thinking it prudent to give the bay a much-deserved rest, Gregory dismounted and led the animal by the reins. They had stopped by a shallow stream not far from the lane to allow the gelding a few sips of the crystal-clear water, when to Gregory's surprise, he spied Eloise Kendall hurrying down the short carriageway of a rather showy new brick house.

She did not see him. The lady walked at a brisk pace, her thoughts apparently a million miles away, and when Gregory caught up with her in the lane and spoke her name, she gasped.

"Your pardon," he said, "I did not mean to startle you."

And startle her he had. When she turned quickly to see who was behind her, her lovely brown eyes were wide with alarm, and her satiny cheeks had turned a vivid pink, almost as if she had been caught doing something reprehensible—something she did not wish anyone to know she had done.

What? he wondered, had the lovely Eloise been up to to bring on that blush?

"Fleeing the scene of a crime, were you, Miss Kendall?"

Since those were the exact words Eloise had muttered not ten seconds ago, she tipped her head downward so the wide poke of her chip straw bonnet would conceal the flush she felt stealing up her face.

"Come, come," he said, falling into step with her, "what have you done? Confess. I have heard it is good for the soul."

Eloise knew he was merely teasing her, and after reminding herself that the two hundred pounds now residing in her reticule was for the good of the village children, she lifted her head and looked directly into Gregory Ward's broad, rugged face. "I have nothing to confess, sir. I do, however, have a question, and I am persuaded you are the very person I should ask."

"Why, Miss Kendall," he said, surprise and amusement mingling in the smile he gave her, "your trust quite unmans me. Pray, ask me anything you like."

Eloise hesitated only a moment, then she plunged right in. "How do you feel about contributions?"

If she had expected him to react with surprise, she was soon disabused of that expectation.

Taking her question seriously, he said, "It all depends upon the contribution. If you refer to money donated for a political campaign or the like, such contributions are a necessary evil. Without them, the wheels of government—and those of charity as well—would soon grind to a halt.

"However," he added, that crooked smile in evidence once again, "if you refer to some *other* sort of contribution—say, a contribution to my personal happiness—I am in complete favor of those." He stopped walking, and she was obliged to stop as well.

"Why do you ask, Miss Kendall? Were you wishful of kissing me?"

"What!"

Aghast at such a suggestion, Eloise thought for a moment that she must have misheard him. However, one glimpse at the light in those green eyes told her she had heard correctly. "Sir! You know I wished nothing of the sort. I would as soon kiss a . . . a tree."

"Really?" he said. "What a waste. I assure you, the tree will not enjoy it. I, on the other hand, would find it quite—"

"I did not say that I *intended* to kiss a tree. I merely meant that I would kiss a tree in preference to kissing you."

He stared at her, as if astonished by her decision. "How very odd. There is, of course, no accounting for taste, but if *I* were asked to choose between kissing a tree and kissing you, Miss Kendall, I would choose you without a moment's hesitation."

He leaned rather close to her then, all teasing gone from his voice, and at his softly spoken words, Eloise felt her flesh go warm all over. "You have such a kissable mouth," he said.

A surprisingly pleasant flutter invaded her midsection. "I . . . I do?"

"Unquestionably. Your lips are full and soft and oh, so tempting."

The flutter spread in every direction, bringing with it a delicious tingling sensation. "They are?"

"Quite tempting," he whispered. "They put me in mind of a ripe, luscious peach, and I should like very much to taste the sweetness of—"

"Sir!" Eloise said, her voice none too steady. "Please, say no more."

"Why?" he asked softly. "Because you do not wish to hear it? Or because you do?"

"Because," Eloise replied, forcing herself to step back a pace so she might put some much needed space between them, "you have passed the line of what is pleasing."

Gregory stepped back as well, and in an instant the teasing light shown once again in his eyes. "*I* have passed the line? Must I remind you, Miss Kendall, that it was *you* who introduced the subject in the first place."

"I never!"

"You said you had a question about contributions, and I merely informed you that a kiss would contribute greatly to my happiness."

"That was not the sort of contribution I meant, and you know it."

His only reply was a chuckle, and the sound made her wish to box his ears.

Angry with him, and furious with herself for having reacted like some desperate old maid to his whispered words about kissable lips, Eloise decided then and there that she could not wait for the coming musicale. She positively longed to see Gregory Ward being pursued by his mama-in-law-to-be. He and the vulgar Mrs. Parker-Smith deserved each other!

Unable to give voice to her feelings, Eloise turned and hurried away, not bothering to wait for him. In her eagerness to leave Gregory behind, she did not watch where she was going, and as ill luck would have it, she stepped upon a small rock, turned her ankle, and lost her balance. She would have pitched forward into the dirt if a strong male arm had not caught her around the waist and held her tight.

"Steady there," Gregory said.

He pulled her hard against his chest while she caught her breath, and as she remained there, relying upon his strength, memories came rushing back to her—memories she had chosen to forget.

It was slightly more than a year ago, the day of Lord Deighton's funeral. The prevailing custom in the neighborhood was for the widow to remain at home while the deceased was laid to rest, so Thea had honored the custom and Eloise had remained with her cousin, to give her whatever comfort she could.

As it turned out, Thea, who had just lost her husband and would soon lose her home as well, was a tower of strength. It was Eloise who had needed comforting.

Lord Deighton had suffered from a lingering illness, yet his death had come as a shock to those who loved and admired him. Eloise had been genuinely fond of Thea's husband, and not just because he had opened his home and his heart to his wife's orphaned cousins.

John Deighton was a good man, and Eloise had enormous respect for him. His death, coming just two years after the demise of her own parents, had opened wounds Eloise had thought healed, brought back heartache she had thought assuaged.

Thea was with the housekeeper, taking care of last-minute details before the funeral guests came back to Deighton Hall for the expected nuncheon, and Eloise, her heart breaking with old and new pain, was in Lord Deighton's library. The smell of tobacco clung to the books on the shelves and to the overstuffed chair John had preferred above all others, and if Eloise closed her eyes, she could almost believe that John was there, in the room.

She stood at one of the rear-facing windows, gazing out at the garden. Tending the roses had been John

Deighton's special joy, and he had pruned and babied the delicate shrubs as though they were the children he had never had.

As Eloise looked at the dozens of rosebushes, their fragrant pink and red flowers in full bloom, she realized that John would never see them again . . . never again smell their heady perfume. The thought had been more than she could bear, and she had sunk to her knees, her forehead pressed against the cool glass of the window, and she had let the sobs come at last.

She cried as she had not allowed herself to cry two years earlier. She wept for her parents. She wept for the loss of dear, kind John Deighton. And she cried for herself—for the carefree girl she had been when the home and family she had known for twenty years had been taken from her.

It must have been the noise of her sobs that covered the sound of his footsteps, for Eloise, believing herself to be alone, gasped with surprise when she felt large, strong hands upon her shoulders.

"My poor girl," Gregory Ward had whispered, his lips very close to her ear.

He had knelt down behind her, and when he put his hands upon her shoulders, to offer her whatever comfort she would accept, she had not cared that there was a history of animosity between them. He was big and strong, just when she needed someone big and strong, and she had relaxed against him, grateful for his strength and his compassion.

He bore her weight as though she were a feather. Her back was against his chest, and it seemed the most natural thing in the world for her to lay her weary head upon his broad shoulder. It seemed equally natural for him to circle his right arm around her waist, while his left arm stretched across the front of her shoulders, the soft wool of his coat sleeve brushing her chin.

They remained thus for an unmeasured time—him with his arms around her, and her with her head upon his shoulder—until her sobs finally abated and her tears ceased to flow. When Eloise raised her head and turned to look at him, to thank him for holding her, Gregory bent slowly and brushed his lips against hers. It was a gentle kiss, filled with tenderness and something else Eloise had never been able to identify, and it was over almost before it began.

"Here," he said, releasing her shoulders so he could reach inside his coat for his handkerchief, "let me see what I can do about repairing that lovely face."

He was drying her tears, his touch soft and unbelievably kind, when the library door flew open so hard it slammed against the wall.

"What is this?"

Perdita Deighton, the new heir's wife, stood in the doorway demanding an explanation, as though the house and all rights were already hers. "Have you so little respect for the recently departed? How dare you behave in this unseemly manner. And here in the man's own library! You are a shameless girl, Eloise Kendall. Utterly, utterly shameless."

Eloise had struggled to her feet, aghast at having been caught in what must appear a compromising situation. Then, like a coward, she had run from the room, leaving Gregory to face the frowning Perdita Deighton alone, to explain to her what had passed between them. He must have made everything right, for Perdita never mentioned the subject again.

As for Eloise, she had put the embarrassing incident from her mind. Until now.

"Are you hurt?" Gregory asked, bringing her thoughts back to the present.

"Release me," she said, remembered embarrassment making her voice sharper than she had intended.

Gregory removed his arm from around her, but he did not let go of her hand. "Can you stand on that ankle?" he asked, concern in his voice. "If not, I can set you on the bay then lead him to the dower house. Nothing easier, I assure you."

Easier for whom? Certainly not for Eloise. Not if she must endure the feel of his strong hands encircling her waist.

Fortunately for Eloise's confused emotions, her injury was not serious, at least not serious enough to warrant her being lifted into the saddle and led back to her home like a child on a pony. Though she walked slowly, favoring the abused ankle ever so slightly, she made it to the dower house on her own terms—terms that required no further physical contact between her and Gregory Ward.

Chapter Six

Gregory left Eloise at the dower house, under the watchful eye of the ever-practical Theadosia Deighton, who promised to see that her cousin propped the injured foot up for the rest of the day. After bidding the ladies adieu until he should see them again in a few hours at the musicale, Gregory mounted the gelding and rode back to Threwsbury Park.

As he neared the gatehouse, he remembered the red deer—if, indeed, that was what he had seen behind the yews—and he decided to stop off and have a good look around. Just to be on the safe side. His uncle had mentioned a band of ex-soldiers being arrested for stealing livestock and poultry in the district, and Gregory wanted to make certain that no one had taken up residence in the old gatehouse.

Lord Threwsbury had referred to the veterans as "worthless vagabonds," and he had expressed a wish to see them all transported to a penal colony. As it happened, the old gentleman was not alone in his opinion, for numerous similarly outraged citizens were calling for mass transportation of the so-called "felonious veterans."

Having been a soldier himself, Gregory empathized with the veterans, and he felt that a far less drastic measure was called for.

The deplorable lot of those soldiers no longer needed for a peacetime army was one of the problems Gregory wished to see addressed by Parliament. Of course, that would take time. Until then, if he should discover that someone was trespassing at the Park, the best he could do would be to give the fellow a few pounds and send him on his way. It was all anyone could do for now.

Unfortunately, when Gregory reached the gatehouse and started to dismount to search the place, his good intentions were sidetracked by the sound of a heated argument. A boyish disagreement was in full swing just up the carriageway, near a stand of hundred-year-old hornbeam trees.

"I want to be Robin Hood!" Basil shouted.

"No!" Jeremy Kendall shouted back. "You got to be Robinson Crusoe yesterday, while I played his man, Friday, so today it is my choice. Fair is fair. I will be Robin Hood, and you will be Friar Tuck."

"I will not!"

"You will, too, unless you fancy a bunch of fives to the bread basket."

"If you mean to hit me," Basil taunted, "you will need help doing it. Better fetch your sister."

The silence that followed this insult told Gregory plainly that debate had given way to fisticuffs, so he forgot the gatehouse for the moment and rode toward the spot where the broad-domed hornbeams gave a suggestion of Sherwood Forest. As he suspected, the boys were rolling around on the ground, grunting and calling each other vile names, but in general doing more damage to their clothes than to one another.

"Pardon the interruption," Gregory said quietly.

The combatants jumped to their feet, obviously surprised to discover they had an audience.

"Sir!" Jeremy gasped. "We did not know anyone was there."

"Cousin," Basil said, his face bright red from combined exertion and embarrassment, "do you mean to tell my grandfather that I was fighting?"

"Is that what that was?" Gregory asked. "Fighting? I vow I have seen better science displayed by the puppets at a Punch Show. What you boys need are a few lessons in the manly art of Greco-Roman wrestling."

Their argument forgotten, both boys rushed forward, begging Gregory to show them a few holds.

"Please, sir," Jeremy said, "that is, if you would not find it a dead bore."

"And," Basil added hastily, "if we need not tell Grandfather."

Gregory dismounted and tied the gelding's reins to a low-hanging branch so the animal could munch upon the sweet-smelling grass, then he returned to the boys. "I will begin," he said, "by showing you how to unbalance your opponent. But first, you two must promise to memorize a quotation for me."

When the boys hesitated, then looked at one another as though they suspected a trick of some sort, Gregory assured them that the quotation was short. "It is credited to Aristotle, perhaps the most intelligent Greek of all."

"Does it have to do with wrestling?" Jeremy asked.

"Indirectly," Gregory replied. "It has to do with friendship, but it might very easily apply to good sportsmanship."

"Very well," Jeremy said, "you have my promise."

"I promise as well," Basil echoed.

"I ask you boys to put the words to memory, because I want you to value the friendship you share. Such closeness is a rare gift, one not easily come by, and I would not like to see it destroyed simply because one of you wishes to win out over the another. Friendship is not about winning, or about who gets what. Aristotle explained it best when he said, 'Friendship is a way of getting pleasure from another's achievements.' "

"Is that all we must learn?" Jeremy asked. "Just that short line?"

Gregory nodded. "Short but powerful. Now, let me hear you repeat it."

With all due solemnity, the boys repeated the words twice; then, after vowing they understood the meaning, they got down to the serious business of learning Greco-Roman wrestling.

"The science," Gregory began, "is in understanding body leverage."

"Body leverage," the boys repeated, their attention fastened upon their instructor's every word.

"And, of course," Gregory continued, "it is a gentleman's sport, so there are no holds allowed below the waist. And no matter the temptation to do so, a fellow may not use his legs to trip his opponent. Is that clear?"

"Yes, sir," both boys replied.

Before long, the youngsters were stripped to the waist and trying their hand at the sport of Greco-Roman wrestling.

Engrossed in giving and in following instructions, none of the three near the stand of hornbeams noticed the little man who slipped from behind the concealment of the yew trees. Beady-eyed, and possessed of a long, thin nose and a prominent chin, the undersized man was decidedly fox-faced, and he moved as quietly as the forest creature he resembled. Creeping past the gates, he hurried down the lane, where he met a large, rough-looking fellow in threadbare coat and breeches and worn-out army boots.

"Whew!" the little man said. "Did yer see the size of that swell who rode in on the bay?"

His companion muttered an obscenity. "Do yer think I got no eyes in me 'ead. 'Course I seen 'im."

Fox Face shuddered. "I'd 'ate ter tangle wif 'im, I would."

"Right," the larger man said. "Which is why I say, we got ter get on wif the business 'fore we get caught. I'm tired of waiting, I am, and if Jack b'aint 'ere by Friday, I say you and me get the dogcart and do the job wifout 'im."

Fox Face took a step back, as if he had been threatened. "Cross Jack? Are you daft, Carl Moffit? I'd as leave jump off the Tower of London. Jack Figby 'as killed men for just *looking* like they was thinking of diddling 'im."

Chapter Seven

By the time the first carriage stopped outside the door of the dower house, Eloise had decided she really must warn Gregory of Mrs. Parker-Smith's plan to see him married to her daughter. Though Eloise still believed that the needs of the children outweighed any guilt she might feel for having taken the bribe, she did not think she could let Gregory walk into a trap unprepared. She had *some* honor, after all.

She and Thea stood at the bottom of the stairs, ready to receive the guests who came for the musicale, and though Eloise had always admired her cousin's ethereal beauty, she had never seen her in better looks than tonight. Tonight Thea was a golden goddess!

Thea's gown was of tawny gold gossamer silk, with a bronze-colored lace trimming the puffed sleeves and the low neckline of the thin, soft-finished satin. Her blond hair was arranged in a waterfall of curls reminiscent of the style favored by the ladies of Ancient Greece, and she had shown her usual good taste by completing the ensemble with a simple gold necklace bearing a single topaz pendant.

Eloise had worn her rose sarcenet, and though she was ten years Thea's junior, she was quite certain that no one would notice her once they set eyes on the Dowager Lady Deighton.

Recalling the seventeen- and eighteen-year-old girls

in white who had shared her disastrous come-out—some of whom had not even shed their baby fat—Eloise wondered, not for the first time, why society pushed young, untried females into matrimony. Far too young to have developed a sense of themselves, the girls were hurried into wedlock before either their taste or their intelligence had a chance to develop.

Looking at Thea, who possessed both beauty and brains, Eloise marveled that society should fail to realize the value of waiting for a woman to mature and come to her full beauty.

As it happened, that wholly unorthodox opinion was shared by the gentleman who was the first guest to be admitted to the house that evening. To say that Mr. Colin Jamison could not take his eyes off Thea was to state the obvious.

"Lady Deighton," he said, bowing over her hand, "you leave me speechless."

"A speechless politician?" the lady replied. "And here was I, thinking that would be an oxymoron."

"Madam," he said, bringing her hand to his lips, "you are as quick as you are beautiful. I see I shall have to be on my metal."

"Be on whatever you like," Gregory said, elbowing his friend aside, "just take yourself off to do it, so that I may greet our lovely hostess."

"Here now," Mr. Jamison protested, "did no one ever tell you that rank has its privileges."

Ignoring his friend, Gregory said, "Thea, you are a goddess, and I worship at your feet."

Thea laughed and bid the gentlemen cease their foolishness. "I would ask you not to put me to the blush in front of my guests."

Since the vicar and his wife were at that moment

being shown into the small vestibule, the gentlemen from Threwsbury Park moved on to Eloise.

"Good evening," Colin Jamison said, taking her hand. "May I hope to have the pleasure of hearing you perform this evening, Miss Kendall?"

Eloise shook her head. "I leave all things musical to Thea."

"And why is that?" Gregory asked, taking her hand in a courteous, if impersonal manner. "Never tell me you are shy, for I will not believe it."

Unaccountably annoyed that Gregory had paid Thea extravagant compliments, while apparently not even noticing her, Eloise said, "Believe what you will, sir. The simple truth is that I am without even a modicum of musical talent."

Thankfully, several guests arrived at once, and the gentlemen were obliged to move away from the receiving line and repair to the withdrawing room, where the paid soloists—a cellist and a violinist—were already seated at the top of the room, tuning their instruments.

As the guests continued to arrive, Gregory and Colin took a turn around the room, introducing themselves to any strangers, and exchanging pleasantries with one or two gentlemen they already knew. When every one of the three dozen chairs was occupied, Thea and Eloise took their places, and the musicale began.

The paid soloists, both of whom were talented artists, performed the first half of the program, which lasted about thirty minutes. After they received their much-deserved applause, there was a short break, a respite in which the guests were allowed to stretch their legs and exchange seating companions if they wished to do so. When the hostess signed that the break was over, the ladies and gentlemen of the neighborhood were invited to share their talents with their friends.

"Lady Deighton!" several gentlemen said at once. "A song, if you will."

When Thea stood and walked to the pianoforte, Gregory slipped into the chair she had just vacated. "How is the ankle?" he whispered to Eloise.

"I am quite recovered, thank you, but I wish you would sit elsewhere. Every time you come near, something happens to me."

"Same here." Ignoring her snub, he patted his chest. "It occurs just here, in the region of my heart. It gets all fluttery. Is that what happens to you as well?"

"It is not!"

"Oh. In that case, it does not happen to me either, and I beg you will forget I said anything."

To Gregory's delight, Eloise was unable to hide the smile that pulled at her lips. "Sir, you are ridiculous."

"What *I* think is ridiculous, Miss Kendall, is for you and me not to enjoy this fine evening. Shall we leave all disagreements for another day?" He held his hand out to her. "What say you, shall we declare yet another truce?"

Since Thea had already begun to play and sing a spirited Italian art song by Scarlatti, her cousin did not reply. She did, however, place her hand in his to seal the pact.

To his surprise, she snatched her hand away after the briefest of contact, and when Gregory looked to see what was amiss, he noticed that Eloise was staring across the drawing room. The object of her attention was an odd-looking female attired in a puce brocade gown and matching turban, an ensemble more suited to a fancy dress ball than to an unpretentious party attended by neighbors.

Even odder was Eloise's reaction to the female. She blushed profusely, while the thin, middle-aged woman nodded complacently, as though the two of them shared a common secret.

The Scarlatti selection was short, and during the enthusiastic applause that followed Thea's performance, Eloise surprised Gregory by employing her fan to hide the fact that she spoke to him. "If you please," she said, "when the music is ended, I should like to make you known to one of our neighbors."

"Of course. I should be delighted. Any friend of yours must be—"

"No," she said, her face even pinker than before, "do not be polite. I assure you, I do not deserve it, for I have done something for which I should be heartily ashamed."

"Should be," he said, "or are?"

"Both."

Nothing more was said, for Thea had graciously agreed to sing an aria from *Cosi Fan Tutte,* and while she performed Mozart's lovely music, her flutelike soprano voice moving with pitch-perfect precision, no one made a sound. At the end of the performance, the burst of applause was both spontaneous and sincere.

During the following moments, when a pretty, young red-haired matron was persuaded to give them the pleasure of a song, Gregory leaned over and spoke to Eloise. "If that act for which you are feeling belated remorse has anything to do with me, there is a way you can make amends."

"Oh?" she said, a suspicious look darkening her lovely brown eyes. "Pray, what way is that?"

"Favor us with a song."

She shook her head. "I do not sing."

"Come now, Miss Kendall, all ladies sing."

"Not *all*, sir."

"Not even for total absolution?"

"Not even then."

"There must be something I can do to make you reconsider. Shall I insist?"

Eloise sighed. "If you insist, sir, I will, of course, sing. However, before I utter the first note, I should like to know if you are in possession of that pocket knife you say you always carry."

Gregory chuckled. "I am, madam. Why do you ask? Is murder on your mind?"

"Not at all, sir. I was thinking of suicide. *Yours.* Once I begin to sing, I promise you, you will wish to cut your own throat rather than be obliged to endure the performance to its conclusion."

He chuckled again. Convinced of her sincerity, he did not insist that Eloise sing. After several ladies, and one or two gentlemen, had performed a few Scottish airs and even a sentimental ballad or two, Gregory suggested that Colin favor them with a song. "A duet," he said.

When the suggestion was seconded by one or two of the guests, the party whip replied that he would be delighted. "If," he said, "Lady Deighton will be so kind as to join me."

Thea did not feign surprise; instead, she went directly to the pianoforte and took her place. While she waited for Mr. Jamison to make his way through the rows of chairs so he might join her, she heard whispers being exchanged nearby.

"On the catch?" one lady replied to the other's question. "If she is, I have heard nothing of it."

"Nor I," replied her confidant. "But she is out of

mourning now, and the gentleman with the mustache is certainly handsome enough to turn a young widow's head.''

Pretending not to hear what was being said, Thea played an arpeggio while Mr. Jamison took his place. He did not stand behind her as she had expected, but assumed a position to her left and slightly in front of her, so they could look at one another while they sang.

One thing at least the gossipers had gotten right; Colin Jamison was handsome enough to turn any female's head. If the truth be known, he was easily the most attractive man Thea had ever seen. Tonight he had forsaken his usual gray for a blue so dark it might almost have been black, and combined with his black hair and eyes, the effect was one of elegance and just a touch of mystery.

As if he read her thoughts, the gentleman with the mustache smiled at her, causing Thea's heart to skip a beat, and warmth to suffuse her face. Hoping her reaction might go unnoticed, Thea began the introduction to the duet.

"Là ci darem la mano," Mr. Jamison sang, and at the sound of his smooth, rich voice, a shiver went through Thea, causing her usually skillful fingers to hit a wrong note. It was as well for her composure that she was obliged momentarily to concentrate upon the keys to avoid losing her place, for it gave her a moment to look away from the gentleman.

She had not expected such deep, velvety tones, and she certainly had not been prepared for the gentleman's superb acting ability. With the first phrase, Colin Jamison took on the very persona of the celebrated Don Juan character, and as he gazed into Thea's eyes, and no place else, she could almost believe he was, indeed, trying to seduce her.

With her heart racing at full speed, she had to keep reminding herself that it was Zerlina, the peasant girl, whom Don Giovanni wished to seduce, and not Theadosia Deighton.

The duet came to an end at last—or was it too soon? Thea was not certain which she felt to be true. Either way, the audience rewarded the singers with a flattering amount of *bravos!* and *bravas!*

"Encore! Encore!" they shouted.

An encore was out of the question, for Thea had only just made it through the planned duet. Considering the erratic state of her emotions, she could not risk a spur-of-the-moment selection.

Without looking at Colin Jamison to see what he wished to do, Thea fixed a smile on her face, closed the instrument, then stood. "Ladies and gentlemen," she said, "refreshments are served in the dining room."

"Lady Deighton," Mr. Jamison said, offering her his arm, "may I escort you to the dining r—"

"No, no," she said. "I cannot—What I mean to say is, I must see to my guests. Please, forgive me."

With that, Thea squeezed past the gentleman and around the pianoforte, then hurried over to join the vicar and his lady. And all the while, her heart kept berating her with, *"Coward, coward!"*

Eloise remained seated, choosing not to add to the congestion caused by the onslaught of guests who slowly exited the crowded drawing room. To her discomfort, Gregory remained by her side. "At the risk of appearing doggedly persistent," he said, "I would really like to know if that action of which you are heartily ashamed has anything to do with the proposed introduction between me and your neighbor."

She had no idea how he had guessed, but she wished he had not used the word, "proposed."

"And," he added, resting his left arm over the back of her chair, just close enough so his thumb brushed the bare skin of her upper arm, "I wonder, as well, if the neighbor in question is that rather peculiar-looking matron in the puce turban."

Had he a crystal ball?

When Eloise would have moved away, he reached across quite unobtrusively with his right hand and caught her wrist, holding it below the level of the chair so none of the guests could see. "Why the sudden wish to hurry away, madam?"

"I . . . I believe Thea needs me."

"Oh, no," he said, "Thea has chosen to flee from her singing partner and has placed herself under the protection of the vicar. Fortunately for her, Colin is a true gentleman, and he would not think of detaining a lady against her will. You, on the other hand, must deal with me, and my manners are not so refined."

Gregory leaned close enough to speak directly into Eloise's ear, and she felt the warmth of his breath upon her neck. It was an unexpectedly pleasant feeling, and though she wished he would keep his thumb still and cease drawing those lazy circles on her skin, she did not move her upper arm out of his reach. As for his hold on her wrist, she was not the least bit intimidated.

"It would serve you right," she said, "if I screamed and caused a scene."

"It is your house, madam. Cause a scene by all means, if that is your wish. But not before you answer my question."

Unaccountably lost in the heady sensations his nearness was causing, Eloise had quite forgotten the question.

"The woman in the turban," he reminded her, as if privy to Eloise's loss of memory. "She has been watching me for the better part of an hour, and if I ever wondered how a tarantula must look while stalking his dinner, I wonder no more. The woman's smile is positively predatory."

Eloise did not even bother looking over toward Mrs. Parker-Smith. The term "tarantula" suited her perfectly, and Eloise could imagine how the spider woman must be envisioning Gregory caught in her web of machinations. "I am sure I do not know what you mean."

"Evasiveness will not serve," he said, "for I want the truth. Has your dislike of me prompted you to sell me into slavery to that man-eating female in puce?"

Eloise was betrayed by the warmth that stole up her neck to color her face.

"Damnation," Gregory muttered beneath his breath, "I spoke in jest. Madam, what in heaven's name have you done?"

"I did not sell you," she said. "Not exactly."

"Not exactly!"

His hold on her wrist tightened, but when Eloise flinched, he loosened his grip a fraction. "Lucky for you, Miss Kendall, that my hands are otherwise employed, for I feel an almost irresistible urge to place them around your throat.

"And I will throttle you," he said, "if you do not tell me immediately what fate has in store for me. Forewarned, as they say, is forearmed, and I have no wish to face the wearer of that puce turban without sufficient ammunition with which to protect myself."

"I vow, Gregory, you are being quite foolish. A big,

strong fellow like you should have no trouble at all in—"

"You used my name," he said.

The softly spoken non sequitur surprised Eloise into looking directly into his eyes. It was a mistake, for his face was mere inches from hers, and as they looked at one another, Eloise felt an unprecedented desire to reach up and touch his firm cheek, to feel the freshly shaven skin against her palm.

Naturally, she did nothing of the sort. She was not some foolish chit who had no idea how to behave in public. She forced her attention from his face, and when she looked away, her gaze settled on Mrs. Parker-Smith, who was even then coming toward them.

"I am sorry, Gregory," Eloise said, "truly I am, but she is coming this way."

"Never mind," he said, giving her wrist a gentle squeeze before releasing her. "As you said, I am a big, strong fellow, and I must outweigh Mrs. Puce Turban a good four stones. If it should come to hand-to-hand combat, I feel reasonably certain I could take her two falls out of three."

At the ridiculous remark, an image sprang to Eloise's mind—one of Gregory and Mrs. Parker-Smith locked in a Greco-Roman wrestling hold. The very notion was too much for Eloise's composure, and she could not suppress a giggle.

"Laugh if you will," Gregory said, "but the woman looks pretty fit to me. It could be a close contest."

Thankfully, the tension between her and Gregory faded away as though it had never been, and by the time the *tarantula* had reached her quarry, Eloise was able to greet her with a semblance of calm.

"Mrs. Parker-Smith," she said, "pray, allow me to

present to you Mr. Gregory Ward, Lord Threwsbury's nephew."

"La, sir," the woman began, her tone embarrassingly overloud and effusive, "I feel as though I know you already, for last Christmas I watched you dance with several of the local young ladies at the Mansfield assembly."

"Truly?" Gregory asked. "How . . . er . . . kind of you to notice me."

"Not at all, sir. Unfortunately, you and I were not then acquainted, so I was denied the pleasure of seeing you partner my dear Sylvia."

She turned and began waving to her daughter, who had remained seated across the room, so she missed the *I-will-have-retribution* look Gregory gave Eloise.

Sylvia obeyed her mama's signal and came forward, but as she drew near, Eloise could not help but notice that for all the money at the Parker-Smith's disposal, poor Sylvia could not have looked dowdier if she had tried. Her gown was overembellished, and the cut of it did nothing to conceal the girl's thin frame; as well, the stark whiteness of the silk called attention to the wearer's regrettably lackluster complexion.

"Mr. Ward," the spider woman said, "allow me to make my sweet girl known to you now."

Gregory bowed to the girl. "A pleasure, Miss Parker-Smith."

Not by so much as a raised eyebrow did he betray the annoyance he must have felt at having been trapped by a social-climbing harridan with little manners and even less finesse, and as Eloise watched him, she was obliged to admit that Gregory Ward displayed more genuine courtesy and good breeding than she had any right to expect.

Employing a fine blend of civility and formality, he

bowed over the hand of the pale, thin young girl who had come running like a frightened rabbit at her mother's bidding. "Did you enjoy the musicale, Miss Parker-Smith?"

Painfully shy, the girl merely nodded, then slipped her bony hand from his noticeably larger one.

"If memory serves," he said, "you were not among this evening's performers. Am I to assume that you, like Miss Kendall, do not sing?"

Though Sylvia sent him a shy smile, her only answer was a shake of her head.

"Naughty puss," Mrs. Parker-Smith said, "speak up, do." Though her words had a teasing sound to them, she glared at her daughter in a way that boded ill for the girl once they left the party.

"Do not stand about like the veriest sapskull, Sylvia. Gentlemen may abhor a chatterbox, but rest assured, they care even less for a chit who refuses to hold up her end of the conversation."

Tears pooled in the girl's eyes, and while she strove not to blink and cause them to course down her cheeks, Gregory was tempted to give the mother the set-down she so richly deserved. He chose not to rebuke her, however, for he was acquainted with enough women of Mrs. Parker-Smith's ilk to know that any censure from him would be visited later upon the hapless daughter. Instead, he asked the timid girl if she meant to partake of the refreshments.

"I . . . I suppose . . . that is . . ."

"If so, may I have the pleasure of escorting you to the dining room?"

When Sylvia gave him a grateful smile that said he had saved her from hours—perhaps days—of scolding and recrimination by her loving parent, Gregory offered her his arm. "I feel it only fair to warn you," he said, "that I am notorious for stealing the sweets right off the plates of my dinner companions. Therefore, if you mean to eat one of the ices, I suggest you take two from the outset."

Rewarded with another shy smile, he led Sylvia away, not bothering to excuse himself to either the girl's mother or to Eloise.

For her part, Eloise took the snub without rancor. If anything, she was inclined to think she had gotten off lightly.

During the half hour that followed, while she dined with Sir Boris Pilcher and listened to an endlessly boring retelling of his investiture the year before, Eloise watched Gregory Ward entertain Sylvia Parker-Smith. The couple sat scarcely two feet way from Eloise and Sir Boris, so it was impossible not to eavesdrop upon their conversation.

It said much for Gregory's address, that on more than one occasion he actually made the shy young girl laugh aloud. Though his manners were relaxed, he never once deviated from the strictest code of conduct, and at no time did he encourage his companion to think his attention was anything more than the sort of behavior expected of any gentleman.

"I never thought to be knighted," Sir Boris said, "but His Majesty would have it that my contribution was worthy of recognition. Still . . ."

Eloise smiled in all the right places, allowing the middle-aged gentleman to prose on to his heart's content, while she concentrated on the conversation taking place between Gregory and Sylvia Parker-Smith.

When the meal finally came to an end, Eloise watched Gregory return Sylvia to her mama. "Thank you," he said to Mrs. Parker-Smith, "for allowing this winsome chit to take pity on an old man."

"Old man!"

So vehemently did the woman deny such a claim that her turban slipped onto her forehead and had to be physically restrained from leaping to the ground. "I never heard such fustian, sir. Why, I am persuaded that any number of young ladies must think you just the right age."

"For a kindly uncle," he said.

When the harridan would have protested further, Gregory forestalled her by reaching over and patting Sylvia's cheek as though she were a child of no more than eight or nine. "And I mean to hold this little girl to her promise to save me a dance when she comes up to town this spring for her come-out."

Having artfully dismissed Sylvia as being too young for a man of his age to take seriously, he completed the picture with his parting comment to the girl's mother. "It has been a delightful evening, ma'am, but I really must take my leave. Lately I have begun to notice that I tire more easily than I used to."

On the pretext of finding his hostess to thank her for a lovely evening, he made good his escape.

Eloise was the last to bid the poor, decrepit soul good night. "You were very good," she said, keeping her voice low so no one else would hear. "I do not begin to know how I am to thank you."

"Do not tax yourself," he said, "for I know exactly how it is to be done!"

With that threat—Eloise could call it nothing else— he bowed over her hand. "Until tomorrow," he said, his tone ominous, "at which time, I shall present you with an entire list of my personal preferences."

Chapter Eight

There had been only three dozen guests at the musicale, but by noon of the following day, it seemed to Eloise that twice that number had come to the dower house to pay calls upon Thea, their avowed purpose to thank her for the party.

"Delightful affair," Sir Boris Pilcher's wife said, while she gathered her gloves and her reticule and prepared to take her leave of the six ladies in the yellow morning room. "But then, your musicales are always delightful."

"Quite," said one.

"To be sure," another said.

"Not to be missed," Mrs. Fitzroy agreed.

"Oh, by the way," Lady Pilcher said before the fifteen-minute visit came to an end, "who is that very handsome gentleman with the mustache? Mr. Jamison, I believe someone called him. A beautiful voice, to be sure, but the man himself, so . . . oh, how shall I put it?. . . *intense*. One might almost think, dear Lady Deighton, that he was making up to you."

"Quite true," Mrs. Fitzroy added. "He appeared very taken with you."

"My dear Lady Deighton, if you will allow a bit of advice from an older, and dare I say it, a wiser head—take care. A young widow cannot be too cautious where her reputation is concerned."

"No, indeed," echoed her companion. "Like silver, a lady's reputation is so easily tarnished. Ergo, it behooves one to keep it unbesmirched."

"Like an old family teapot?" Eloise suggested.

For the entire morning, Thea had been obliged to endure similarly phrased "advice" from well-meaning neighbors, and she had chosen to answer each of those impertinences with complete silence.

Eloise, on the other hand, lacked her cousin's patience with such unmitigated meddling, and by the time the tenth visitor had come, put in her tuppence worth, then departed, Eloise was ready to explode. Thus it was, that when the new Lady Deighton, traveling by coach and pair for the negligible distance separating the manor house and the dower house, chanced to touch upon the subject of Mr. Colin Jamison, Eloise had reached the limit of her endurance.

"I thought it best," Perdita said, "since Charles and I are your nearest relatives, that I offer you a bit of adv—"

"Your pardon," Eloise said, "but Jeremy and I are Thea's nearest relatives. Her mother and mine were sisters, which makes us first cousins by blood. You and Lord Deighton, on the other hand, are merely second cousins by marriage."

Perdita, bristling as though insulted by the clearing up of their various relationships, chose to speak directly to Thea. "Be that as it may, my dear Thea, I thought a hint was in order regarding your behavior last evening."

"A hint?" Eloise said. "What a novel approach. We have endured so much *advice* this morning that a mere *hint* must be a refreshing change."

The lady of the manor ignored Eloise's interruption.

"To put it bluntly, my dear Thea, your conduct was unseemly."

When Eloise would have protested, Thea silenced her with a look.

"I do not say this to hurt you," Perdita continued, "but that duet was nothing short of scandalous. I vow, the entire village can talk of nothing else. Even those who were not here to witness the embarrassing display are carrying the tale."

Furious that anyone should take it upon themselves to censure her cousin's behavior, Eloise said, "I pray you, Thea, pay no attention to the spiteful old cat!"

Their guest gasped. "Old cat! How dare you speak of me in such—"

"Perdita is just jealous," Eloise continued.

"Jealous?" The new Lady Deighton laughed, though the sound lacked conviction. "What foolishness. I have no reason to be jealous of Thea."

"Oh, yes, you have. You may be the wife of the heir, and you may possess the house and the title, but you will never replace Thea as the neighborhood's primary hostess, and you know it."

"Eloise," Thea said quietly, "I assure you, this is not necessary."

"Yes, it is. Perdita is envious of your beauty, your talent, and your popularity with the neighbors, and if the dower house were not legally yours for life, by way of the marriage contracts, I daresay she would have flung you out upon the street the day after John's funeral."

"Well! Of all the rude—"

"Furthermore," Eloise continued, "I would ask you, Perdita, how you can possibly know what tales are being bruited about in the village. Unless, of course, you were up before dawn, going from house to house to insure that everyone got the word about—"

"Eloise!" Thea interrupted. "That is quite enough. Please, my dear, say no more."

Quite certain she could not curb her anger if she remained in Perdita's presence a moment longer, Eloise quit the morning room, slamming the door as she went. She slammed the entrance door as well, threatening every last windowpane, and as she ran across the carriageway and hurried toward the stone footbridge, where the gently flowing water of the brook offered a quiet haven, she vowed to spend the remainder of the day sitting upon the phlox-covered banks if necessary, until the final busybody had come and gone.

While Eloise sought solitude, Mr. Colin Jamison, blissfully unaware that his impassioned duet of the evening before had inspired a flurry of busybodies to descend upon Thea, joined his friend in the smaller of the two dining rooms at Threwsbury Park. Lost in thought that brought a smile to his face, he took a gold-rimmed plate from the stack at the end of the hunt board and served himself a basted egg and a muffin. "Gregory," he said, "I am glad I found you, for there is something I wish to tell you."

"Mm hmm," muttered his friend, only half listening. Gregory had taken the gelding out for a long, hard ride before coming to break his fast, and his primary interest at the moment was in discovering the source of the mouth-watering aromas coming from the dozen or so covered dishes laid out before him.

Apparently not in the least discouraged by Gregory's lukewarm reception, the gentleman in gray continued. "By this time tomorrow," he said, "I hope you may be wishing me happy."

It needed a moment or two for the significance of

the announcement to penetrate Gregory's thoughts, which had become centered on choosing between kippers and shaved ham. "What did you say?"

"I said that I hoped by—"

"Yes. I thought that was what you said." After carefully replacing the silver lid on the chaffing dish, Gregory looked directly into his friend's face, as if to see for himself if the man was in earnest. "You are serious about this?"

"Quite serious. I mean to call upon Thea Deighton this very evening. At which time, I shall ask her to be my wife."

"This is all very sudden, my friend. Do you tell me you have formed a *tendre* for the lady?"

Mr. Jamison nodded. "How could I not? She is the most divine creature I have ever met."

"I will not argue the point, for Thea is, indeed, a lovely person, both inside and out. I knew you were interested in her, Colin, but I must ask you, has she given you cause to believe that she shares your sentiments?"

The gentleman pressed his finger against his mustache. "Let me say only that she has not spurned my friendship."

"She would not, of course, for Thea is a truly generous person. However, she—No," he said, "I will not interfere in something that is none of my business. It is your life—and Thea's, if she chooses to accept your proposal—and the last thing you need is someone else putting their oar in."

Gregory walked over to the mahogany dining table, set his half-filled plate at a place set with ornate silver cutlery, then turned to his friend, his hand outstretched. "I will say only this, that I applaud your excellent taste. Any further comment will keep until after you have spoken to the lady."

"Fair enough," Colin said, shaking the proffered hand.

While the two gentlemen broke their fast, then lingered over cups of rich, fragrant coffee, Colin spoke at length about the lovely and intelligent Thea Deighton. Gregory was in complete agreement about Lady Deighton's many admirable qualities, but the subject that most occupied his thoughts was the possible upheaval this marriage might cause in the life of the lady's cousin, Eloise Kendall.

If Thea should accept Colin's proposal of marriage, what would become of Eloise? Colin Jamison, though politically and socially successful, was not a wealthy man. He did not even own a home, for he had found that bachelor rooms in town perfectly suited his needs. Those rooms were ample rather than spacious, and though a wife might move into the limited space with little or no difficulty, there would not be room enough for a wife *and* two extra cousins.

Would Eloise be forced to move elsewhere? Even if Thea possessed a life interest in the dower house and agreed that Eloise might remain there, a single female could not live alone without a chaperon in residence. Paid chaperons were easy enough to come by, of course, if one had sufficient money to afford them. Did Eloise's inheritance produce enough income to allow her to hire such a person? Did she have funds enough to enable her to maintain a staff and continue to live in the style to which she was accustomed?

Gregory's concern for Eloise was still uppermost in his mind later that morning when he took a turn in the earl's formal garden. He had gone outside in search of fresh air and solitude, but when he turned a corner of the meticulously planted herb and flower garden, he was surprised to discover Mr. Everett Browne, young Basil's tutor.

The Scotsman sat upon a wrought-iron bench situated at the end of a crushed stone path, and he was reading what appeared to be a letter. When he looked up at Gregory's approach, tears filled his pale blue eyes, giving evidence that he was much moved by the words he had just read.

"Your pardon," Gregory said. "I had no notion anyone would be here."

Mr. Browne jumped to his feet and bowed politely. "It is I who should beg your pardon, sir. After all, you are a guest of the house."

"While you, Mr. Browne, are a resident, and must claim precedence over one whose visits number in the days."

The young man blushed to the roots of his fiery red hair. "As a paid resident, sir, my duties do not include sitting about in the gardens."

Gregory raised his hand as if swearing an oath. "If you do not tell, I shall not."

The tutor smiled shyly. "Actually, sir, I should be returning to Basil and Jeremy, for by now they will have finished translating today's passage from the writings of Plutarch." He looked once again at the paper in his hand. "I came outside merely to read my letter."

"Then do so, by all means. I will walk in some other direction, for I should not dream of invading your privacy."

"You are very kind, sir, but the contents of the letter will not be private for very much longer." His voice quivered on the final word, and unable to keep his emotions in check another moment, the young

Scotsman pulled a brightly colored handkerchief from his pocket and buried his face in it.

Though Gregory knew that sentimentality was all the rage among some of the more poetic young men, *he* was not comfortable with it, and he looked all around him, any place but at the weeping tutor. While Gregory tried to think of some way to extricate himself from this particularly embarrassing scene, the Scotsman pulled himself together and dried the tears from his face. "Your pardon, Mr. Ward, but as a result of this letter, you see before you the happiest of men."

If this was happiness, Gregory hoped never to be around when the fellow was in the doldrums.

"Actually," Mr. Browne continued, "as soon as matters can be arranged, I hope you will be wishing me happy."

Since those were almost the same words Colin Jamison had spoken earlier, Gregory said, "Do I understand you, Mr. Browne? Are you telling me that you are engaged to be married?"

"Aye, sir, I am that. Since Michaelmas, when I asked the young lady for her hand, and she did me the honor of accepting my proposal."

"I had not heard."

"Nor has anyone, sir, to my regret. Due to circumstances quite beyond my control, we could not marry straight away, and for the time being the engagement had to remain private between the lass and me."

Gregory drew breath to give voice to the appropriate words of congratulation, but the tutor spoke first. "All appeared hopeless until this morning, when I received this letter from Miss Kendall, delivered to me by her brother."

"Miss Kendall!" Gregory would not have been more surprised if the fellow had walked over and attempted to knock him down. "The letter you are weeping over is from Miss *Eloise* Kendall?"

"Aye, sir, and what she has proposed for my future has made me the happiest of men."

"The devil you say!"

"Oh, you need not tell me, sir, that I do not deserve such good fortune. I realize that the secrecy surrounding my betrothal does not speak well for my character, and believe me, that was never the way I wished to do the thing. Unfortunately, at that time there was no other way for the lady and me to pledge our devotion to one another except in strictest privacy.

"With Basil going off to school next year," he continued, "and my employment as his tutor coming to an end, my prospects were not brilliant. Miss—my fiancée—is an orphan, without a dowry and with neither older brother nor uncle to advise her, so it remained for me to be strong and postpone the marriage until I found further employment."

The tutor's eyes filled with moisture once again, and he was obliged to use his now sodden handkerchief to wipe away the unmanly display.

While the fellow swiped at the tears, Gregory experienced an almost uncontrollable desire to grab the sentimental moonling by the collar and throttle him until his teary eyes popped right out of his head.

Gregory was consumed by rage! Rage so intense he thought he might choke from its effects upon his heartbeat and his breathing. Eloise, secretly engaged? And to this . . . this sniveling, carrot-topped young puppy?

No! It could not be. There was some mistake. Eloise would not choose a man like Everett Browne. Her personality was too strong to allow her to find happiness with such a partner. If Gregory was any judge of the matter, the spirited lady would be unable to tolerate this watering pot for an entire day, never mind a lifetime. Given her temperament, she would probably murder the fellow within a fortnight.

Eloise Kendall needed a man whose temperament matched her own. An equal. One who would stand up to her and enjoy the give and take of the confrontation. She needed—no, she deserved—a man who knew how to please a woman whose veins flowed with fire. She deserved someone who understood the subtleties needed to awaken the passions that lay sleeping just beneath the surface of the cool, self-contained Miss Kendall.

Devil take it! Everett Browne was totally wrong for Eloise! She needed a different sort of man altogether. She needed a man like Gregory.

Staggered by the absolute, undeniable truth of that revelation, Gregory turned without a word and left the garden, his destination the stable. If he did not put some distance between him and Mr. Everett Browne, he would surely do away with the presumptuous puppy, murder him before Eloise had the chance to do it.

Besides, Gregory needed to see Eloise. Immediately.

The potential murderess had remained at the bridge for the better part of two hours. Three more coaches had arrived, each depositing their occupants at the dower house, where they might call upon Thea, but because Eloise had not yet gained control of her anger, she deemed it best not to rejoin her cousin.

For a time she sat on the bank of the brook, filling the dragging minutes by picking individual blossoms from the bright pink phlox and using them to weave

a bracelet and an accompanying ring, which she
donned upon completion. She had very nearly finished
a double strand necklace, when the childish occupation palled. Bored from inactivity, and out of patience
with her nosy neighbors, Eloise began to wish the entire population of Mansfield Downs might be transported on the instant to Hades. "And good riddance
to the lot of them."

"Do I interrupt?" the Reverend Underwood asked.

Eloise gasped, for she had not heard the kindly old
gentleman approach. Happy she had not given voice
to her wish to see the entire neighborhood suffering
the fires of Hades, she said, "You never interrupt,
Vicar. Please, join me."

She got to her feet, brushed the flowers and the
unfinished necklace from the lap of her lavender muslin frock, then joined the white-haired vicar on the
bridge.

"When my good wife expressed her wish to drive
over to thank dear Lady Deighton for last evening's
most enjoyable musicale, I took the opportunity to
accompany her so that I might speak to you."

The vicar took Eloise's hands in his, ignoring the
phlox bracelet that circled her left wrist and the bright
pink ring that adorned her finger. "My dear child,"
he said, "I cannot begin to communicate to you the
joy I felt this morning when your maid arrived, bringing me your letter and the pouch containing the two
hundred pounds."

"There is no need to tell me of your feelings, Vicar,
for I am persuaded they were much the same as my
own when I first received the money."

"What a splendid contribution. Only think what we
can do with so much money."

"I have though of it, sir. In fact, at the same time

my maid was en route to the rectory to deliver my letter to you, Jeremy was delivering another letter to Mr. Browne, at Threwsbury Park, asking the tutor if he was still interested in being second schoolmaster at the village school."

"Very efficient of you, my dear. Will the young man accept, do you think?"

"I have every reason to believe he will be pleased to accept my offer, for he once let it slip that he has an understanding with a young lady from his village in Scotland."

"Engaged to be married? That is excellent news, to be sure, for a husband and wife will lend added stability to the school."

"I thought so as well," Eloise replied.

"Do I understand correctly?" Gregory Ward said, surprising both Eloise and the vicar by his sudden appearance, "that the purpose of the coming marriage is to gain stability for your school?"

The vicar was the first to respond. "I daresay young Mr. Browne's motives are somewhat more personal but I hope that Miss Kendall and I will be forgiven for our own rather shortsighted view of the coming nuptials. After all, she and I have worked for two years to realize our dream of a village school. And now that we have the funds to see us through the first year, we are doing whatever it takes to see that the dream becomes reality.

"Whatever it takes," Gregory repeated.

Eloise might have questioned Gregory's sudden interest in the tutor's personal affairs, had her thoughts not been wholly taken up with watching the tall gentleman as he walked the final few yards to the bridge. For a large man, Gregory Ward moved with unexpected gracefulness.

"Hello," she said. The word sounded suspiciously breathless to her ears, but if either gentleman noticed, they did not show it.

Though Eloise had not admitted it even to herself, part of the reason she had waited at the brook was so she might see Gregory alone. She had not forgotten his parting words to her last evening when she had tried to thank him for enduring Mrs. Parker-Smith's toadying and for being so kind to poor, mousy Sylvia. He had said he knew exactly how Eloise could thank him, and he had warned her that when he saw her the next day, he would present her with an entire list of his personal preferences.

When he had said it, something in his eyes—a speculative look that was totally male—had awakened a heretofore unknown response in Eloise, and she had lain awake for most of the night, recalling the frisson of excitement his words and that look had engendered. In the quiet darkness, she had pondered with unexpected pleasure just what his preferences might be.

She had wondered as well if, when they met on the morrow, he would make good his threat. And if his idea of a proper "thank you" involved some sort of physical retribution, would she attempt to stop him?

Only when dawn approached, painting the night sky with her gold and pink brush strokes, did Eloise finally give up her fruitless guessing game and fall asleep.

Bringing her thoughts back to the moment, Eloise realized that the vicar had continued to speak, and that she had heard none of what he had said. "How she induced Mrs. Parker-Smith to part with so much money," he said, "I cannot begin to guess, but I am persuaded our dear Miss Kendall was on the side of the angels."

Eloise felt the heat of embarrassment, for she knew

the angels had nothing to do with that particular bargain, and from the look Gregory gave her, he was of a similar opinion.

"And now," the kindly old vicar said, "you young people must excuse me. I promised to join Mrs. Underwood at the dower house, and she will be wondering what became of me." Smiling as though at a joke on himself, he added, "A wise husband does not keep his wife waiting for too long, as our Mr. Browne will soon discover."

He took Eloise's hand in his and patted it as though she were a child. "We will speak again tomorrow, my dear Miss Kendall."

"Yes, Vicar," she replied. "Tomorrow."

After bidding Gregory a pleasant afternoon, the Reverend Underwood took himself off, leaving Eloise to make what she could of Gregory's scowling countenance. Though why he should be scowling now, she had no idea. Surely he had guessed last evening the sort of promise she had made to Mrs. Parker-Smith in exchange for the two hundred pounds, so why was he looking at her as though he would like nothing better than to shake her until her teeth rattled?

"Come," he said, "you and I need a bit of privacy, and this place is as busy as a posting inn."

The words were not unlike what she had supposed he might say, but the tone was all wrong. The man was definitely angry, and when he took her by the arm and led her toward the deeply cut dale that bisected the lush green pasture land that was part of the Deighton Hall estate, his grip was anything but romantic.

Romantic!

Astonished by the thought, Eloise stumbled, and she would have fallen if Gregory had not been holding her arm. Had she lost her reason? Surely she had not truly expected today's encounter to be romantic. Or had she? Foolish beyond permission, of course, for Gregory Ward was the man she liked least in the entire world. He always had been.

Romantic indeed. She must have drunk more champagne last evening than she had realized to have come to that particular conclusion.

As for Gregory, it was obvious from his attitude that he had something quite different in mind.

Not a little embarrassed by the direction of her foolish thoughts, Eloise let Gregory lead her down the sloping land to the bottom of the dale before she pulled her arm free of his rather punishing grasp. "This is far enough, sir. Whatever you have to say to me, it cannot require more privacy than this pasture. Unless, of course, you fear one of the sheep will cease to graze and take up eavesdropping."

He said nothing, just continued to walk, and to Eloise's surprise, she caught up with him, then kept pace with his long strides as they crossed the bottom of the dale then continued up the far side. Still without saying a word, they strolled toward a low stone wall and crossed over the wooden stile. Finally, using a quieter tone, Eloise said, "Gregory, tell me, what is this all about?"

"I was with Mr. Browne earlier," he said, the words forced through straight, unsmiling lips. "He received your letter."

Gregory seemed to expect her to say something. What, Eloise could not imagine. "Yes?"

"The fellow had the audacity to inform me that you had made him the happiest of man."

"He did? Excellent. Then he must mean to accept my proposal."

Gregory muttered a mild obscenity, and though Eloise heard it, she decided to let it pass, deeming it unwise to ring a peal over a gentleman when he was so obviously out of temper.

As if coming to some sort of decision, Gregory stopped walking and turned to look at her. "This marriage," he said, "is a mistake. You must know that no good can come of it. And certainly no happiness."

Eloise sighed, exasperated with Gregory and with his totally illogical mood. Of what possible interest could the tutor's future be to anyone but himself and his fiancée? Was this some special day Eloise had not heard about, a day in which everyone had been granted freedom to mind everyone else's business?

"I do not know," she said, "if the marriage is or is not a mistake. However, I cannot think that Mr. Browne's happiness concerns anyone but him and—"

"Devil take it, Eloise! I have no interest in what befalls the tutor. The fellow can go to Hades, for all I care. It is *your* happiness I wish to discuss. *Your* marriage."

"M—my marriage?"

Eloise was taken completely by surprise; rendered speechless. Gentlemen did not discuss marriage with a young lady, not unless . . .

Heaven help her! Was this the way Gregory meant her to thank him? In a million years Eloise would not have guessed that matrimony was one of the things he had wished to discuss with her. And certainly not while in this most unloverlike mood.

Without so much as a by-your-leave, he caught her left hand and glowered at the ring she had fashioned of phlox blossoms. "Damnation," he said, tearing the bright pink circlet from her finger, "you deserve better than that."

Matrimony? Rings? These were heady topics, indeed, and any young lady could be forgiven if her heart began to pound rather painfully against her ribs. Unsure what to say, in light of Gregory's ever-growing temper, Eloise tried for a teasing tone. "Of course I deserve better. A big, vulgar emerald comes to mind, surrounded by half a dozen equally vulgar diamonds."

Gregory was not amused. His response could only be called a snort, and a derisive one at that. "You have sorely misjudged your man, Miss Kendall, if you think he will supply you with emeralds and diamonds."

He? Why was the maddening creature speaking of himself in the third person? Something was not quite right here, and Eloise had endured just about enough of Gregory's temper and this very odd conversation. Was he proposing to her, or was he not?

"You may consider yourself fortunate, Miss Kendall, if the fellow buys you a simple gold band."

"The fellow? Gregory, I find I am having a difficult time following your thought processes. Would you just say whatever it is you wish to say to me and be done with it?"

"As you wish, madam. If it is forthrightness you prefer, forthrightness you shall have. You are making the mistake of your life."

"I am?"

"Certainly you are. You cannot marry a man you do not love."

"I cannot?"

"Of course not. And if you mean to try to bamboozle me into believing you have a *tendre* for the fellow, you may save your breath. To love such a sentimental fool, you would need to be as stupid as he, and your other faults not withstanding, I have never believed you to be stupid."

"You have never believed—" This was too much. "If that is your idea of a compliment, Gregory Ward, allow me to inform you that it falls short of the mark. Now have done, I beg of you, and tell me in plain English what this is all about."

"It is about you," he said, "and that cursed man milliner."

"What cursed—"

She got no further, for Gregory caught her by the shoulders and pulled her toward him—so close that her face was mere inches from his. He said nothing for several heart-stopping moments, merely looked at her, and Eloise was certain he meant to kiss her.

Of its own free will, the tip of her tongue came out and moistened her lips, and as Gregory watched the slow circling movement, the anger in his eyes ebbed away, and something else took its place—something that made his green orbs appear darker, and quite deliciously intimate, as though they searched Eloise's very soul.

No man had ever looked at her like that. The look was at once frightening and exciting—and as heat slowly engulfed her, deep inside her some primal female feeling sprang to life, as if it had waited a long time to be awakened by the right person.

Eloise was just adjusting to the idea that Gregory was, indeed, that right person, when he let her go and stepped back.

After a moment of strained silence, he said, "For the love of heaven, Eloise, think what you are doing."

"I do not want to think," she said, her voice so husky it did not sound like her own. "I merely want to be k—"

"No! Do not say it. You cannot want to marry Everett Browne."

Chapter Nine

Eloise felt as though someone had played a cruel hoax upon her; as though they had offered her a warm toddy, then thrown icy cold water in her face instead.

"Marry Everett Browne? Me? Is that what this is all about?"

"Of course. What else?"

What else, indeed?

At that moment, Eloise could not decide which feeling was strongest within her, incredulity or mortification. On the one hand, she was amazed that anyone could think she would even consider marrying the shy Scotsman; while on the other hand, she knew a feeling of intense embarrassment for her totally wanton reaction to Gregory.

She had practically thrown herself at him, believing that he wanted to kiss her, to marry her; while Gregory had wanted nothing more than to warn her against entering into a mésalliance. He had told her to think what she was doing, and she had very nearly begged him to kiss her. Thank heaven he had stopped her before the words were spoken.

How could she have misread his intent? How could she have been so foolish to think that Gregory Ward had come to make her an offer of marriage, when their entire history was one of animosity?

"Do you deny," he said, "that you and Everett Browne are engaged?"

"Most emphatically. Wherever did you get such a preposterous notion?"

"From your letter."

"Never. If that is what you thought, you cannot have read the missive very carefully."

"Read it?" he said, apparently insulted by the suggestion. "I do not read other people's correspondence."

"Perhaps you should. Had you done so in this instance, you would not have come over here acting like some deranged person."

"I did not act like a—"

"You did," she said. "Quite deranged, and all for naught. Had you taken the time to read my letter, you would have seen that it said nothing of marriage. In the missive, I merely asked Mr. Browne if he would like a position as schoolmaster. I proposed a salary of fifty pounds per annum, plus rooms above the school, and—"

"You *proposed* a salary of fifty pounds."

"That was the sum mentioned. Unfortunately, we can afford no more than fifty. I would have liked to offer him more, for he wishes to marry a girl from his village in Scotland, but . . ."

She paused, for Gregory was shaking his head. "A girl from Scotland. Not you?"

"Certainly not me."

If she had not jumped to enough conclusions for one day, Eloise would have sworn that Gregory's face showed a hint of red beneath the tan.

"Miss Kendall . . . Eloise, I cannot believe what a muddle I have made of this entire episode. I have acted quite stupidly, and I promise you, I mean that as no compliment. Can you forgive me for acting like a . . . a—"

"Deranged man?" she offered.

He laughed, though there was as much self-derision as humor in the sound. "Go ahead. Flay me. I deserve it."

"Yes, you do. In all fairness, though, I cannot help but think this misunderstanding is my just reward for having taken that bribe from Mrs. Parker-Smith."

"The contribution?"

"Bribe. Call it what it was. Honesty compels me to admit that I discovered a lack of character on my part—one I had not known existed—for I agreed to serve you up to the woman as a sort of sacrificial lamb. Had I shown more character and refused the money, none of this would have happened."

"True," Gregory said, "but neither would you have your two hundred pounds, the needed schoolbooks, and a second schoolmaster. All in all, I think more good was done than harm. That is, if you can forgive my rather bone-headed error about Mr. Browne and—"

She held up her hand to silence him. "Please, let us not go there again. What say you that we forgive one another and do our best to forget—forget everything save a pleasant musicale and a donation that has enabled the vicar and me to do some good for the children of Mansfield Downs?"

Gregory offered her his hand to seal the bargain. "Forgive and forget," he said. "I have always believed that a selective memory is the key to harmonious human coexistence."

Eloise placed her hand in his, and though the feel of his rough palm against hers reminded her of that delicious sensation she had felt when she had thought he meant to kiss her, she put the memory aside. "To harmonious coexistence," she said.

They had walked farther than either of them had realized, so by common consent they turned and retraced their steps. When they came to the stone wall, Gregory went over the stile first, then he turned and assisted Eloise to climb up the wooden steps. When she would have jumped from the final step to the ground, he put his hands at her waist and lifted her down.

As soon as her feet touched the soft grass of the pasture, she expected him to let her go. When he did not do so, but gazed rather intently into her eyes, Eloise felt that warmth steal over her again. Surely, this time he meant to kiss—

No! No! Make sport of me once, shame on you. Make sport of me twice, shame on me.

Recalling the old adage just in time, Eloise stepped back, obliging Gregory to release her. "Come," she said, "Thea has no idea where I have got to, and she may be concerned." Having said this, she turned and walked rather hurriedly toward the dale.

Gregory caught up with her in a matter of seconds and took her elbow to assist her, lest she encounter a hare's hole and trip. "All this talk of marriages," he said, as though the moments at the stile had not happened, "puts me in mind of something I wanted to ask you."

No! Eloise was not falling into that trap a second time either. Choosing her words carefully, she said, "What, precisely, do you wish to ask?"

"If Thea should wed," he began, surprising Eloise with the turn in conversation, "where would you live? Could you go up to the Hall, to the new Lady Deighton?"

"Live under Perdita's roof!" Eloise closed her lips upon a decidedly unladylike word. "Never."

Gregory chuckled. "Burned that bridge, have you?"

"To cinders," she replied. "And even if I had not, I should as soon go to the workhouse."

"The workhouse! Surely things are not as bad as all that."

"Of course they are not. I am not wealthy by any means, but my father left me with enough money so that Jeremy and I need never be in want. Besides, Thea has no intention of marrying, and the dower house is open to me for as long as I have need of it."

"Are you so certain that Thea wishes to maintain the status quo?"

"Really, Gregory, this is too much. First you believed that I was engaged, now you have me homeless and Thea on the verge of remarriage."

"I admit to having been a bit cork-brained in my assumptions about you and Mr. Browne, but believe me, that is not the case here. I am merely interested in your welfare."

Eloise rolled her eyes heavenward. "I vow, you are as bad as those interfering old cats who have been invading the dower house since early morning. How could you allow one little duet to mislead you into jumping to such an illogical conclusion?"

"Is it so illogical?" he asked quietly.

"Of course is it."

"And yet," he said, "I know it to be true that Colin Jamison is in love with Thea."

"In love?" Eloise shook her head.

"I know as well," he continued, "that Colin means to make Thea a declaration this very day."

When Eloise made no reply, Gregory said, "I do

not say this to upset you. I meant merely to give you a bit of advance warning."

Eloise remained silent.

"Surely you have seen the looks that pass between the two of them when they believe no one is watching. I am persuaded theirs was a case of love at first sight."

"No, you are wrong. I would have noticed if something like that was happening."

"Would you? I wonder."

Gregory gave her a look she did not understand in the least. "We all have our flaws, Eloise, and yours is that you allow past experiences to seriously color your interpretation of present circumstances."

"What does that mean?"

"You are an intelligent lady," he said, "think about it. And when you have thought it through, let me know."

At the moment, Eloise's brain was too filled with conflicting emotions to make sense of his cryptic remark. He was wrong about Thea and Colin Jamison. It was not true. It could not be. Eloise had certainly noticed the way the gentleman looked at Thea, especially during that infamous duet last evening, but Eloise had seen no reciprocation from Thea.

Or had she?

Staggered by the possibility that Thea had feelings for Mr. Jamison, and suddenly bombarded by understandably selfish fears about what changes this would bring about in all their lives, Eloise struck out at the only target available—Gregory Ward. "Thea would not *dream* of remarrying," she said. "You are just saying that to get back at me, and I think you are detestable."

With that, she pulled her arm free of his grasp and hurried away. Gregory caught up with her, of course, with his long legs he was bound to overtake her, but during the remainder of the walk back to the brook and thence to the entrance door of the dower house, Eloise refused to enter into further conversation with him. Her thoughts were wholly taken up with Thea. Her cousin would not accept Mr. Jamison's proposal, Eloise was certain of it.

And yet, the seeds of fear had been planted.

"Thea," Eloise called the moment she entered the dower house, "where are you?"

"Up here," Thea replied, "in my bedchamber."

Eloise hurried up the narrow stairs to her cousin's pretty lilac and silver bedchamber. To her relief, Thea sat at the dressing table. With a small scissors held in her right hand, she calmly trimmed a broken fingernail on her left, as though making the repair was the most important thing on her mind.

"You were gone a long time," Thea said. "I am pleased to see that you are still with us, for I had begun to think you might have fallen off the face of the earth."

"And if the neighbors had not finally stopped coming," Eloise replied, "I might have wished for such a fate."

Eloise strolled over to one of the front-facing windows and perched on the edge of the padded window seat. "Forgive me for deserting you, Thea. Was it terribly tedious, with everyone bent on making you a gift of their unsolicited advice?"

Thea did not answer the question; instead, she contented herself with, "You were wise to play least in sight."

"I went to the brook. I suppose Reverend Underwood told you that he met me there."

"He did tell me. The dear man was so pleased about the plans for the school, that he could talk of nothing else."

Ignoring that topic, Eloise plunged into the one that was foremost in her thoughts. "I suppose the vicar informed you as well that Gregory Ward was with me at the brook."

Thea looked up from her nail repair, a teasing smile on her face. "Since I can see for myself that you are as dry as a bone, I assume Gregory was not up to his old tricks."

"New tricks," Eloise said, trying for a casual tone. "I spoke with him at length, and, Thea, he said the most preposterous thing about Mr. Jamison. You will laugh when I tell you what it was." Eloise forced a laugh, but her cousin merely stared, while a slight blush turned her cheeks pink.

"According to Gregory," Eloise continued, "Mr. Colin Jamison has formed the intention of calling upon you this evening, to . . . to . . ."

"To do what?" Thea asked quietly.

Eloise swallowed to relieve the tightness in her throat. This conversation was proving more difficult than she had expected. "He means to make you a declaration."

Thea's blue eyes widened in surprise, but immediately she returned her attention to the small scissors in her hand. "A declaration? You are quite certain that is what Gregory said?"

"Quite certain. According to Gregory, Mr. Jamison told him that he was in love with you."

When Thea did not comment, Eloise said, "I told you it was preposterous. As though someone could be in love in less than a week. Why, you and John knew

one another for three years before you wed. Now, that
was love. John would never have—"

"John was my husband," Thea said, "and I loved
him dearly. But his way was not the only way. If he
were here, he would be the first to tell you, and me
as well, that people may love differently at different
times in their lives. Furthermore, I . . ."

Eloise held her breath. "You what, Thea?"

Her cousin laid the scissors on the dressing table
then stood and walked to the bedchamber door. "I
need some air."

"Do you want company?"

Thea shook her head. "Pray, do not be offended,
my dear, but I have had more than enough company
for one day. Right now, I need to be alone. To think."

"About Mr. Jamison?"

Eloise did not miss the flash of anger in her cousin's
eyes, though it came and went quickly. "I . . . I am
sorry, Thea. I had no right to pry. You will say I am
no better than that gaggle of geese who paraded
though here this morning."

"I will say nothing of the kind."

"But you would think it, am I right?"

A halfhearted smile was Thea's only answer. After
a brief wave of her hand, she turned and descended
the stairs, and within a matter of seconds she had
exited the house, closing the entrance door softly behind her.

Once outside, Thea chanced to see Angus, Perdita's
black-and-white terrier, running down the carriageway
toward the lane. Since Thea had no destination in
mind, she went in pursuit of the little dog, who had
escaped from the Hall for perhaps the hundredth time.

"Not that I blame you," she said, following the animal into the lane. "I recall a few occasions when I wished to escape the Hall myself."

Feeling decidedly disloyal, she bit her bottom lip to stay the tears that burned at the back of her eyes. Thea had loved her husband, for John Deighton was kindness itself, but he was also a man who thrived on the quiet country life, finding contentment in his books and in his rose garden.

Unfortunately, there had been times during the years she was married to John, when Thea had felt stifled by the calmness of their existence. An insightful and well-informed woman, she often longed for some occupation that would challenge her intellect—something of more importance than arranging vases of flowers for the Sunday church service and playing hostess to the same neighbors year after year.

Not that she had ever let John know she was not content with her lot. What would have been the point in telling him?

A kind-hearted man, had he known of his wife's boredom, the knowledge would have made him miserable as well. And yet, he could have changed nothing. For the most part, there were two kinds of women in the world: those whose lives were filled with drudgery and the endless struggle for survival; and those, like Thea, who were asked to do only one thing—to marry and supply their husband with an heir.

And Thea had not even accomplished that task.

Perhaps, if she been madly in love with John, she might have been content to spend her life as his wife, devoting all her energy to him and to nothing more. Unfortunately, she had loved her husband, but she had never been *in* love with him.

Last evening, when Colin Jamison sang the opening lines of their duet, and Thea looked up into his handsome face and those dark, mysterious eyes, she knew for certain that she had never been in love. Not until that moment.

"But is that enough?" she asked.

Catching up with Angus, she swooped the little dog into her arms and looked into his sad, brown eyes, as if hoping he might have the answer to her question. "I ask you, my boy, is being in love merely an emotional opiate designed to deaden our reason and convince us that we must devote our lives to the person whose nearness makes our heart race and our breath come in short gasps?"

"Yip, yip."

"Is it real, this being in love? Or is it just nature's way of inciting humankind to mate and stay together long enough to rear their young?"

"Yip, yip, yip."

"You are much too quick with your answers, Angus, old boy. It makes me wonder how much I can depend upon your wisdom."

With the terrier still in her arms, Thea began to stroll along the low stone wall that divided the lane from the Deighton Hall property. If she had hoped to leave her confused thoughts behind, however, she was soon disabused of that notion. Visions of Colin Jamison dogged her every step.

"What am I to do, Angus?"

When Thea had thought Colin Jamison was just some romantic figure who would pass out of her life as easily as he had come into it, she had embraced her infatuation, allowing herself to enjoy the pleasurable sensations for once in her life. To be in love was exciting stuff, especially when she believed the object of her affection would be gone in a few days. Such love required no commitment on her part. No risk to her heart. No gambling with the rest of her life.

Now, however, she had been informed that the man who set her temperature soaring planned to make her an offer of marriage. Marriage. Commitment. Thea had not thought of it going that far.

Why was it that everyone else believed they knew what was best for her regarding her behavior and her life, while she, the person most involved, shook like a blancmange when faced with the actual decision. She was a grown woman; it was time she took command of her own destiny. But did she want to? Did she want to risk giving her heart to another man?

John had been a wonderful husband, dear and kind, but their relationship had never brought Thea the excitement, the passion she had dreamed of. Was this her chance at true happiness? Was Colin the love of her life?

All she knew for certain was the way she felt when he was near. She felt alive. Filled with excitement. With hope. With anticipation. If she married Colin Jamison, life would never be safe or predictable. And truth to tell, that knowledge scared Thea right out of her wits.

Angus, who had seemed content in Thea's arms, began to bark, his high-pitched *yippity-yip-yip*, warning her that a horse and rider galloped down the lane.

The rider was Colin. Thea could not see him yet, for the horse had not rounded the bend in the lane, but she knew it was Colin. The accelerated beating of her heart told her it was him.

Moments later the horse appeared, the same black gelding Colin had ridden the day they went to Creswell Crags, and just watching the magnificent animal

and the equally magnificent rider come closer set
Thea's senses on fire.

"Hello," Colin said, tipping the stone-colored beaver that was a perfect compliment to his pearl gray
coat and the slate blue breeches.

"Hello," she replied.

Colin did not dismount immediately; instead, he
turned slightly then leaned forward in the saddle, so
he might look into her upturned face. He smiled, and
Thea was unable to still her own lips from responding
in kind.

"Because you would have no way of knowing it," he
said, "I feel it my duty to apprise you of something."

"And that is?"

"That yours is the most beautiful smile in all of
England."

Thea laughed. "The entire country?"

"No question about it."

"I see, sir. And you have seen that many smiles,
have you?"

"Oh, yes. Being a politician, I have traveled from
John O' Groats to Land's End, and from the Isle of
Man to Dover, and in those travels I have clasped at
least ten thousand hands and witnessed twice that
many smiles. But I promise you, not one of those
smiles rivals yours."

"Prettily said, sir, but I take leave to doubt the accuracy of such a sweeping claim."

He dismounted and, with the gelding's reins in
hand, came to stand just in front of Thea. "If you are
questioning my veracity, lovely lady, I really must be
allowed an opportunity to clear my name."

"Pray, how is that to be accomplished?"

He spoke very softly. "I can think of only one way."

Thea held her breath. She longed to hear the words, and yet, she had never been more frightened.

"Shall I tell you how it may be accomplished?" he asked.

"How?"

Her question was barely audible, but he heard it, for he stepped even closer to her, and when he spoke, his voice was soft and low, and the timbre of it sent a shiver down Thea's spine. "I could take you there," he said. "To all those places and beyond. Far beyond. I should like to show you the Greek islands, if it would please you to see them."

Thea's heart beat painfully in her chest. She wanted to tell him to stop, to say no more, but she said nothing.

"You would love the islands," he whispered. "Especially Crete, where bright yellow sunshine warms the white sand beaches by day, and by night the silvery moonlight kisses the dark blue waters of the Mediterranean. Let me show you," he said. "I know a private cove that is the closest thing to heaven on earth, for the soft, gentle air caresses the skin like magic, and the water is so inviting you will be unable to resist the desire to bathe in the—"

"No, really. I—"

"Go with me, beautiful Thea. Go with me, and I promise you smiles and joy and untold delights."

"Sir. You must know I cannot go to Greece, or to the Isle of Man, or to . . . to any of those places. It is impossible."

With his free hand, Colin lifted Thea's fingers to his lips. "My sweet," he murmured against her skin, "nothing is impossible. Not if you love—"

"No. Please. Do not say it."

"I beg of you, my love, do not forbid me to say what is in my heart."

"I must."

"But why? Is it me? Have I misjudged your feelings? My own are so strong, perhaps I mistook the situation. Do not spare me, Thea. If you do not love me as I love you, tell me so directly, and I shall say no more. I have no wish to distress you, so if you cannot care for me, I will go. I should hate to leave, but I will do so."

"I . . ." Thea could not say the words. She could not tell him that she did not love him. She could not give voice to words her heart told her would be a lie. She did love him, never more so than at this moment, with him so close, his lips teasing her fingers, and his dark eyes searching for the truth in her eyes, mesmerizing her with the passion he did not try to conceal.

Her senses reeled at the idea of moonlight walks with him, of bathing in the sea with Colin beside her, his strong arms around her, holding her close. His mouth upon hers. She thrilled at the very thought of the two of them together day and night. Oh, the nights. Thea had no doubt the nights would be pure magic.

And yet . . . how could she be certain that what she felt was not some aberration—some abnormality of nature, like a night flower that comes to life suddenly, is gloriously beautiful for a few hours, then with the coming of the sunlight, dies as quickly as it bloomed. Eloise was right, Thea had known Colin only a matter of days, and with so short an acquaintance, how could she possibly know if what she felt would endure the test of time.

And what of Eloise? Eloise and Jeremy were Thea's only remaining family, and she loved them. Recalling the distress she had seen in Eloise's eyes, how could Thea desert them for some dream of romance?

Too confused to know what to tell Colin, she removed her hand from his gentle clasp. "Why must I give you my answer right this moment?"

"Because, my sweet, I am bound for London tomorrow. I must be back in town on Monday for a very important meeting with the Prime Minister, and I should like to leave here knowing that our plans—yours and mine—are settled. You will learn that I am not a man given to rash decision, but I am a man of action. Once I have decided what is the right thing to do, I do it. I love you, I know that to be true, and I do not need six months or a year to be certain of my feelings."

"But this has all happened so fast. Too fast."

"Not for me," he said. "I have waited forty years to find you, Thea, and I want to spend the next forty years with you by my side. I want to learn all there is to know about you. What makes you laugh. What makes you cry. All the things that make you angry.

"And," he added, the softly spoken words sending a shiver of delight though Thea, "I want to know how you like to be kissed. How you want to be held. Touched. And above all, I want to discover what makes you purr with contentment."

"I . . . I am sorry," Thea said at last, the words very nearly choking her.

Colin closed his eyes for an instant, effectively concealing his reaction from her. "Are you telling me, Thea, that you do not love me?"

No! Never! "I am telling you," she said, "that my head is spinning, and that I cannot make a serious commitment on such short acquaintance."

"Is that to be my only answer? I ask you if you love me, and all you can say is that your head is spinning?"

At the sharpness in Colin's voice, Angus came to life in Thea's arms and began to bark as though he believed she was under attack.

"Colin, please, I—"

Lifting his voice above the dog's increased barking, Colin said, "I would have an unequivocal answer, Thea. Will you marry me? Yes or no?"

Thea shook her head. "I am sorry, Colin, but if you must have an answer right this moment, then it will have to be no."

Chapter Ten

"Well," Lord Threwsbury said upon seeing his guest, Colin Jamison, gallop past them on the carriageway, his destination the Hall, "I am certain the fellow must have seen us, yet he pretended otherwise. What do you suppose has your friend in such a temper?"

From the scowl on Colin's face, Gregory did not need more than one guess. The party whip had obviously put his luck to the test, and Thea had refused his offer.

That made two of them who had gone off half-cocked today. First Gregory succeeded in making Eloise despise him yet again, then Colin made a premature proposal to Thea. For supposedly intelligent men, he and Colin looked suspiciously like a pair of lummoxes.

"Never mind him," Lord Threwsbury said, "I want to see if the bailiff was correct. If someone has broken into the gatehouse, I want them arrested. I'll have no trespassers on my property. A groat will get you a guinea, my boy, that the trespasser is one of those soldiers turned vagabond you are so keen on mollycoddling."

"Save your money Uncle. First, let us see what the bailiff has to say. There is always the possibility that he could be wrong."

Gregory had volunteered to come in his uncle's place, mainly because he felt guilty about not investigating the gatehouse yesterday, when he thought he saw someone behind the yews. His lordship, not surprisingly, had refused to stay at home, but when he called for his fowling piece, Gregory had insisted upon accompanying the old gentleman, just to make sure that no one was injured.

As it turned out, one of the gatehouse windows was, indeed, broken, and the front door stood ajar. However, the floor of the two rooms belowstairs was strewn with packed leaves and animal droppings, and the mess was more likely the result of mice or squirrels than of some two-legged creature.

"All the same," his lordship said, "I mean to send a note to Squire Munson. Not that he will be at home where he belongs. Always gallivanting someplace or other with that flibbertigibbet wife of his. What is the point in having a Justice of the Peace, I should like to know, if the fellow is never at home to keep the peace?"

Gregory saw no point in arguing, so he volunteered to keep watch that night, to set his uncle's mind at rest that no trespassers would gain entrance to the estate. "If anyone tries to break in this evening, sir, be he a veteran or not, I promise to apprehend him and turn him over to the squire without delay."

That evening, Thea declined supper, sending a message down to Eloise that she had the headache. Actually, the excuse was not far from the truth, for after she had refused Colin Jamison's proposal, Thea had come home and sought refuge in her bedchamber, where she had spent the remainder of the day in bed weeping. As a consequence, the misery she felt was as close as made no difference to being a headache.

What was in a name? Headache? Heartache? None but the sufferer could appreciate the distinction.

The case clock at the top of the stairs had already chimed nine times when someone tapped softly at Thea's door. Thinking it was her maid, Thea lifted the damp cloth she had placed over her face and called out, "Go away, Mary, do. I told you I did not want anything to eat."

"It is I," Eloise said. "Please, Thea, may I come in?"

The previous two times Eloise had tapped at the door, Thea had remained silent, pretending to be asleep. Unfortunately, having already spoken, she could do nothing this time but admit her cousin. "You may come in," she said, "but I promise you, I do not wish to talk."

"I know," Eloise said, opening the door and stepping inside the bedchamber. "I am sorry you do not feel well, Thea, and I vow I will not stay above a minute, for I do not wish to add to your distress. However, my mother used to say that for families to be successful, the members must never allow the sun to set upon an argument."

"Did we argue?" Thea asked, returning the wet cloth to her face.

"As near as makes no difference. For that reason, pray allow me to apologize for anything I said this afternoon that may have angered you. I had no right to comment either for or against Mr. Jamison, or to try to influence you in any way. I was wrong, and I beg you will forgive me."

When Thea remained silent, Eloise drew a loud breath then let it out slowly, as if to fortify herself for further penance. "You, and you alone, know what is right for you, Thea. If you have formed a *tendre* for the gentleman, then allow me to be the first to wish you every happiness."

Thea still said nothing, and Eloise cleared her throat, her embarrassment evident. "I admit to having been persuaded by my own selfish interests, and I implore you, Thea, not to let my situation influence you against your own best judgment. Naturally, I shall miss you, but I am persuaded I will be fine on my own. I . . . I want you to be happy."

Thea lifted the damp cloth again and looked directly at her cousin. "Happy? I doubt I shall ever know such a state."

"Whatever do you mean? I thought . . . that is, I assumed—"

"Your assumptions not withstanding, Eloise, I fear I have made a complete shambles of my life. Due to my lack of courage, Colin has now taken me in dislike and is probably preparing to leave for town as we speak."

Even if Mr. Jamison did mean to leave, Eloise would not allow his departure to be Thea's fault. "No matter what has happened between you and the gentleman, you are the most courageous person I know."

Thea shook her head in denial. "I am a coward."

"Never!"

"It is true. I refused Colin's most flattering offer because I could not convince myself that to marry him would insure my happiness. And wise or foolish, I take full blame for my actions. I made the decision."

Eloise looked at her cousin's pale face and swollen eyelids and knew she had been weeping. "And do you tell me that you are now regretting the choice you made?"

"How can I say? All I know with any certainty is that my heart is broken."

Eloise stepped toward her cousin, her purpose to offer what sympathy she might. "My poor dear, you—"

"No," Thea said, "do not. At this moment, the last thing I want is sympathy. From anyone. Do not be concerned for me, I beg you, for I shall survive this heartbreak as I have survived others."

"Thea, perhaps it is not too late to—"

"In the meantime, Eloise, I would appreciate it if you, and others of my acquaintance, would stop assuming that you know what is in my best interest. It may have slipped your notice, but I am a woman grown, and for that reason, I am perfectly capable of deciding my future for myself . . . and of living with the consequences."

While a chastened Eloise tiptoed from her cousin's bedchamber, Gregory Ward moved silently toward the broad-domed hornbeam trees to the left of the Threwsbury Park carriageway. Once he had found a likely spot, hidden from possible prying eyes, he made himself as comfortable as possible on a low joint stool, stretching his long legs out in front of him and resting a holstered saddle pistol across one knee. From the cover of the tree, he kept watch the entire night for anyone who might try to enter the gatehouse.

Had Gregory but known it, the miscreants for whom he watched had other plans for the evening. The two who had been loitering near the gatehouse were back at Creswell Crags, inside one of the many small limestone caves.

As they had done the other nights of that week, the large man with the threadbare coat and worn-out

army boots, and his small, fox-faced companion had
lit a meager fire, and in the confined space of the cave,
the smoke from the fire burned their lungs and made
their eyes fill with tears. Still, the flames offered the
only warmth available, so the men sat beside that pitiful, smoking pile of logs eating the last of a scrawny,
roasted chicken and guzzling from a jug of blue ruin.
All around them, on the floor of the cave, lay bones
from past, unsatisfactory meals.

Once every morsel of chicken had been consumed,
the two men sat in morose silence, passing the jug
back and forth, as if hoping the cheap gin might take
the edge off their discomfort and their impatience.
They had waited an entire week for their leader, the
infamous Jack Figby, to join them, and still he did
not come.

"Devil take it, Lew," said the large, rough-looking
fellow, "where's Jack?"

" 'E'll be 'ere, Carl. Try for a bit of patience."

"I'm tired of being patient, and I'm sick of waiting.
I'm cold, and me belly's so empty it thinks me throat's
been cut."

"Hush," the little man said. "Bad luck ter talk
about such things."

"Like bad luck don't dog us at every turn. Why, we
wouldn't know good luck if it was ter come up and
bite us on the arse. Tomorrow's Friday, and like I told
yer before, if Jack b'aint 'ere by Friday, I say we get
the dogcart and do the job wifout 'im."

The little man turned quickly toward the mouth of
the cave, to assure himself that no one lurked there
to overhear their conversation. "And I told you, Carl,
that I b'aint crossing Jack Figby. A big feller like you
'ud 'ave a chance against 'im, but not me. Jack 'ud
slit my gullet for just thinking of playing 'im false."

The big man cursed then spat on the ground. "Yer a little weasel, Lew Rolf, and that's a fact. Yer got neither cod nor beggars' bullets, and even if yer 'ad 'em, you wouldn't know ought ter do with 'em."

"I got bullets aplenty!" Fox Face said, ready to defend his impugned masculinity. "But I still b'aint crossing Jack."

"A wise move," said an emotionless voice from the darkness just outside the mouth of the cave. "Mayhap you'll live to see another day."

"Jack!"

The two men beside the fire jumped to their feet, and as the newcomer, a medium-sized man with a pale, nondescript face and cold gray eyes, walked slowly toward the firelight, Lew Rolf began to back away, his ugly little face contorted with fear. His partner, on the other hand, remained beside the fire, and though he stood his ground, he took a large pull off the jug of gin.

"Dutch courage?" Jack asked quietly. "You'll need it."

Though the large man muttered an obscenity, his gaze did not quite make it up to the newcomer's cold gray eyes. "Yer late, Jack Figby, and me and Lew 'as decided ter go it alone."

"Not me!" the little man called from the rear of the cave, his high-pitched voice sounding disembodied in the darkness.

"We done all the work," Carl continued, "and we don't need nobody coming along now ter take the lion's share of the money."

"Don't listen to 'im, Jack. Carl's just jug-bitten is all."

"Oh," he said slowly, "is that it?"

"Yeah, Jack, that's it. Carl and me been having a

little nip to keep out the cold, but we been waiting for you and doing just like you told us. I got the dog-cart hidden away so don't nobody find it, and I been watching the Park every day, seeing who comes and goes until I ken the lay good as I ken Soho or the Stews. You can trust me, Jack. As for Carl, don't pay 'im no 'eed. 'E's drunk, and 'e don't know what 'e's saying."

"Doesn't he?"

Carl lifted the jug and took another gulp of the blue ruin. "Drunk I may be, but I mean what I say. I'm done taking orders."

"Now that," Jack Frigby said, "is most unfor-tunate."

Figby stepped nearer the smoking fire, his hands in the pockets of his greatcoat, as though to keep them warm, then when he was no more than a foot from Carl, he stopped. "So," he said, "you're sure you're done taking orders?"

Carl, fully a head taller than Jack, straightened his shoulders, as if to emphasize his greater size. "I'm sure. Me and—"

He got no further, for Jack whipped his right hand out of his pocket, and quick as lightning punched it into the larger man's belly.

Carl made an "Oomph!" sound—just that, nothing more. The jug slipped from his hand, and for several moments he stood quite still. Then, he grabbed his middle, doubled over, and collapsed onto the filthy, bone-strewn earth. Once he hit the ground, he did not move again, and he made no further noise.

Jack Figby moved slowly as though he had all the time in the world. After placing his booted foot against the fallen man's shoulder, he pushed him onto his back, revealing the hilt of the knife protruding from Carl's stomach. Leaning forward, Jack yanked the long, slim blade free, then he wiped the steel across the sleeve of the dead man's threadbare coat. Once the blade was dried to his satisfaction, Jack folded it back into the handle and returned the weapon to his coat pocket.

"Gorblimey!" Lew cried. "You killed 'im. You killed Carl."

Jack Figby turned to look at the man who had begun to whimper. "You want some of the same, Lew?"

"N—no, Jack. Please. You got no call to kill me. I done everything like you told me."

Figby, his eyes two blocks of cold, unyielding ice, stared at the trembling man. A full minute passed, then finally he said, "You got anything more you want to say about this job?"

Lew Rolf shook his head with such force it threatened to fly off his shoulders. "I got nothing ter say. Nothing at all. Honest. I'm yer man. You can count on me, Jack. I'd never even think of betraying you."

"Then quit your jawing and get this carcass out of here."

"Yes, Jack," the little man replied, his voice trembling with fear. "What yer want I should do wif 'im?"

After retrieving the jug the dead man had dropped, Figby wiped his palm across the earthenware neck to remove any dirt particles. He hoisted the jug to his shoulder, took a long, deep swallow, then pointed to Carl. "Roll him over the edge of the cliff, " he said. "The carrion birds will do the rest."

While Lew Rolf tried to figure out how he was to drag the lifeless body of his partner across the rough ground, Jack Figby tossed the jug aside, then sat in the exact spot where Carl had sat only two minutes ago. After taking a spill from the fire and using it to light a cigar, Jack inhaled deeply of the burning tobacco, then let the pungent smoke drift slowly out his nostrils. "Ahh," he said, "there's nothing more relaxing than a good cigar. Don't you agree?"

Using the back of his hand to swipe at the tears that trailed down his thin, scraggly cheeks, Lew said, "Right you are, Jack. Nothing more relaxing than blowing a cloud."

Lew's knees shook so badly they threatened to give way beneath him. He was terrified of this cold, emotionless man; more frightened of him than of anything else in his life. He feared Jack Figby more than he had feared the Frenchies with their fixed bayonets, and even more than he had feared his drunken old pap, who had knocked his undersized, defenseless son about repeatedly for doing nothing more than breathing.

Too intimidated to do anything but obey Jack's command, Lew caught hold of Carl's legs and began to pull the much larger man through the mouth of the cave.

"Get a move on," Jack said, "and when you've finished, bring in my horse. He's tied just outside. While you rub him down, you can tell me everything you've learned about Lord Threwsbury's grandson."

Chapter Eleven

"**I** won!" Basil shouted. "I bested Jeremy at last. He outweighs me by a stone, but I finally pinned him."

Lord Threwsbury's grandson lay across his friend's shoulders, having successfully wrestled the larger boy to the ground, where he held him for a count of three. At last, after receiving the tap on the back that indicated the end of the match, Basil got to his feet and began to dance around on the grass, hooting and shouting in boyish glee.

Gregory let him enjoy his victory for a few moments, then he said, "Have done, Basil, there's a good lad."

"But I won! I won!"

"True enough, and I applaud your victory. Nevertheless, an important component of Greco-Roman wrestling is learning to be a good sport."

"I was a good sport," the boy said. "Every time Jeremy pinned me, I congratulated him. And now that I have finally been the victor, I am congratulating myself."

There was more Gregory could have said on the subject of good sportsmanship, but in all fairness, he could see the boy's point. Perhaps Basil was entitled to a few moments of crowing.

After offering a hand up to Jeremy, who still sat on

the ground, Gregory praised both boys for having
shown real aptitude for the sport. "I wish there was
time for more lessons," he said. "Unfortunately, Mr.
Jamison and I must leave tomorrow, for we have
important business in town on Monday."

"Aw," Basil said. "Just when I was getting good."

Jeremy did not complain; instead, he made Gregory
a very polite bow. "Thank you, sir, for taking the time
to teach us a few fundamentals. Next term, when Basil
and I go to school, if we are lucky enough to earn
places on the wrestling team, we will owe it all to
your instruction."

"Not so, lad. In wrestling, as in everything else in
life, a person earns their place as a result of three
things: their willingness to practice, their ability to
learn from their mistakes, and their determination to
stick with their dream even when success seems out
of reach."

He gave each boy a playful right jab to the chin.
"Now get back up to the Hall," he said, "before Mr.
Browne comes in search of you. I should hate to have
him ring a peal over me for having kept you from
your books for too long."

The boys laughed aloud, diverted by the thought of
their spindly-legged tutor ringing a peal over as prime
a specimen of manhood as Gregory Ward. Once they
had donned their shirts and coats, however, they
thanked Gregory, then the three of them walked up
the carriageway to the Hall.

Upon entering the vestibule, Gregory discovered
Colin Jamison descending the grand staircase. The
party whip, looking his usual debonair self in a coat
of pebble gray over a striped silver waistcoat, was followed by one of the earl's footmen, who carried the
gentleman's valise.

Taken by surprise, Gregory said, "What is this?"

"Ah, Gregory, there you are. I hope you will forgive me, but I have decided to leave for town this morning."

"This morning? But our plan has always been to remain until tomorrow. Can you not wait another twenty-four hours, so that we may travel together as scheduled?"

Colin shook his head. "I should prefer not to wait. The butler informs me there is an inn in the village where a decent post chaise can be hired, and I find I am more than ready to be back in town, in my own rooms."

Gregory had no trouble dating this sudden desire to be in London to Thea's refusal of Colin's marriage proposal, and while he wished his friend would wait another day, he would not try to dissuade him from going. "If that is what you feel you must do, at least allow me to drive you to the village."

"Now that offer," Colin said, "I will accept."

While Gregory went abovestairs to change his shirt and freshen up, the chestnuts were put to and the phaeton brought around to the front of the house. Colin had taken his leave of Lord Threwsbury that morning, so without further delay, the two gentlemen took their places for the short trip to the village inn where the chaise was to be hired.

As they drove down the carriageway, past the gatehouse, and out onto the lane, what little conversation passed between the two friends was mostly political. Gregory took care not to introduce the subject of Thea Deighton, but when the chestnuts trotted past the entrance to Deighton Hall, he noticed that Colin Jamison spared a moment to look over his shoulder at the charming, multiwindowed dower house. Gregory looked as well. Since neither of the ladies was taking the air in the rustic garden, both gentlemen returned their attention to the lane.

"I suppose," Colin said, "that at some time during the day you will be taking your leave of Miss Kendall and her cousin."

"It was part of my plan. Have you any messages for Miss Kendall or the dowager Lady Deighton? If so, I should be happy to deliver them."

Colin hesitated. "Actually, you might tell Lady Deighton that I . . ."

"That you . . ." Gregory prompted.

Colin studied a speck of dust on the thumb of his right kidskin glove. "No," he said at last, "there are no messages. I am persuaded that everything has been said between us."

Gregory took leave to doubt it, but keeping to his vow to mind his own business, he merely nodded.

Considering his vast experience with the fair sex, Gregory could have given his less-seasoned friend a bit of sound advice that might have smoothed over the misunderstanding between him and Thea. Unfortunately, Colin sought no such guidance.

If what Gregory suspected was true, his friend, in his enthusiasm to declare his love, had seriously rushed Thea Deighton, and had not given her time to get used to the idea of being courted. Like spirited horses, females were often skittish at first, and they liked to be given time to get used to a fellow.

When it came to affairs of the heart, the sexes approached the matter from totally different directions. Once a man knew he wanted to marry a particular female, he was inclined to want to get through the preliminaries as quickly as possible and get right to the "I do's" and the wedding night.

Conversely, females took uncommon delight in the preliminaries. They wanted the rides in the park; the bouquets sent around to the house; the alfresco breakfasts. To rush a female through the courtship was to deprive her of experiences and memories she would cherish for a lifetime.

As well, a female needed time to get to know her intended—time to be certain of her heart before giving it, her fortune, and her future into one man's keeping. Females had a lot to gain socially from marriage, but in general they took the bigger risk.

Gregory felt compassion for his friend. After having waited for years for the right woman, Colin had laid his love at Thea's feet, only to have that love rejected.

Or so he believed.

Gregory had every confidence that Thea returned Colin's feelings, and that she had rejected not the gentleman but his approach. Colin had moved too fast, and like a skittish horse, Thea had bolted and fled.

Amateurs! Where politics was concerned, Colin Jamison might be the downiest fellow in the nation, but when it came to women, he had a lot to learn.

As do we all!

If the truth be known, Gregory's celebrated expertise with the fair sex fell by the wayside every time he was in Eloise Kendall's company. What a muddle he had made of his visit yesterday. A bull let loose in a parlor could not have left more chaos in his wake.

When Gregory and Colin reached the inn, located at the top of the high street, it did, indeed, have a chaise for hire, and within a matter of minutes the inn yard became a bustle of activity. While a team of horses was selected and put to the chaise, the post boy who would ride the lead horse came forward, bowed, and made himself known to his temporary employer. Once all the preparation was completed, Colin and Gregory shook hands and promised to talk Monday evening, after Gregory's meeting with the Prime Minister.

"Until then," Gregory said, after which he closed the chaise door and stood aside, watching until the vehicle carrying his friend disappeared down the road that led to London.

The dust had not yet settled when Gregory's thoughts turned to the drive back to Threwsbury Park—a drive that would take him past the dower house once again. He had planned to take his leave of the ladies later that afternoon, but upon second thought he decided that now was as good a time as any.

Though custom decreed that he do no more than leave his calling card—one for each lady—with "P.P.C." written on the white pasteboard to let the ladies know he was leaving the neighborhood, Gregory hoped to be invited inside the house. Eloise might still be angry with him, and choose not to be "at home," but surely Thea would receive him. At least he hoped she would. Once he was inside the house, Eloise might decide to speak with him after all.

Since Gregory's mind was occupied with planning what he would say to Eloise if she should receive him, he did not hurry the chestnuts; instead he allowed them to travel the lane at a leisurely pace. Even so, within little more than a mile their speed was sufficient to overtake a dogcart pulled by a lumbering, dun-colored mare whose advanced age and swayed back explained her slow pace.

Like the mare, the dogcart had seen better days. In all probability, it had never been much of a cart, for it consisted of little more than an unpainted plank seat with pen space beneath for four hunting dogs. At the moment, the pen space was empty. Someone had tied a wide, rolled canvas to the back of the plank seat—presumably to let down in case of rain to protect the dogs—and if Gregory was any judge of the matter, the canvas, which appeared to be new, was probably worth more than the horse and cart combined.

It was not to be wondered at that Gregory's high-bred cattle should take exception to following such a nondescript animal and such lowly equipage, and if the truth be told, Gregory was none too pleased to be eating the other vehicle's dust. Unfortunately, at that point a low stone wall hugged the lane on the left side, so he was obliged to hold the chestnuts firmly in check until they found a spot where the lane was wide enough to allow them to pass.

That spot was reached at last, and Gregory was able to give the pair the office to advance. As the phaeton drew alongside the dogcart, Gregory glanced at the two men on the plank seat. He was acquainted with neither the driver nor the subdued little man who sat beside him. Since his visits to Mansfield Downs were never of long duration, however, it was not to be wondered at that he did not recognize everyone in the area.

They were an odd-looking pair. The driver was of medium build with a surprisingly pale complexion for a country laborer, and his companion was a small, wiry-looking fellow with a sharp, protruding profile. Somehow, they seemed out of place in the country, for they neither looked up nor waved, but kept their eyes downcast, reminding Gregory more of the type one saw moving furtively through the alleys and side streets of London.

The driver wore an old brown felt hat whose shapeless brim concealed half his face, and when Gregory lifted his hand in greeting, the fellow touched his finger to the brim. The action was not so much a salute as it was an opportunity for the man to pull the brown felt down even further around his face.

Somehow, the word "clandestine" sprang to Gregory's mind, but he dismissed the idea as pure foolishness. What possible business would a pair gallows birds have in a quiet village like this? Obviously Gregory had let his uncle's talk of vagabonds and poultry thieves distort his judgment.

A far more plausible story was that the driver had sustained some facial injury during the war and was merely concealing the disfigurement from prying eyes. Whatever his reasons for not wishing to be seen, they were his business and no one else's.

Gregory put the matter from his mind, for within moments he was obliged to give his attention to his horses. The pair began to step lively, and in a very short time the phaeton had left the dogcart and the two strange-looking men behind.

As it turned out, Gregory was not obliged to leave his card at the dower house, for Eloise answered the door herself. "It is you," she said.

"As you see," he replied, stepping inside the vestibule.

If she had planned to offer some excuse for absenting herself, it was too late now, for having come face-to-face with him, she could not claim the headache or some other malady. Besides, she looked too healthy for such excuses. Dressed in a sprigged muslin frock whose sleeve inserts and square neck were trimmed in cherry red grosgrain, she put Gregory in mind of a field of poppies.

Gregory had always thought Eloise pretty, even when she was a child, but now that she had given up the pastels worn by young girls and had adopted the full, rich colors that complemented her dark hair and brown eyes, she was absolutely stunning. Lord, but he would love to take her to town and put her in Mademoiselle Lisette's capable hands. Dressed in the height of fashion, Eloise Kendall would be an incomparable.

A burgundy opera cloak with a sable fur collar would suit her coloring to perfection. As would a tawny gold silk evening dress trimmed with russet lace. Or a shimmering, emerald green satin ball gown.

Or a negligee in hyacinth blue.

At the thought of Eloise clad in a flowing negligee, Gregory felt his cravat positively shrink around his neck, threatening to choke him. An instant later, the image of the beauty not *in* the negligee, but *out* of it, rendered another article of his clothing much too snug for comfort.

Not since his adolescent days had the mere thought of a woman pushed Gregory to the point of embarrassing himself. What was worse, he suspected that it was not *a* woman, but this *particular* woman who had the power to tie him in knots.

Eloise Kendall, the spirited child who had kicked him in the shins on his twelfth birthday, had slipped into and out of his life at different periods, but never once had she left him without some reminder of her existence.

What was it about the cursed female?

True, she was beautiful, but Gregory could name a hundred women whose faces were more striking. And though her figure was curvaceous and totally feminine, he had known, and bedded, at least a dozen females who were more voluptuous. By her own admission she possessed no musical talent, and if her inability to get along with the new Lady Deighton was any indication, Eloise did not always do those things that were in her own best interest.

If the truth be told, neither her accomplishments nor her amiability merited more than a passing nod. And yet, no other woman had ever taken possession of Gregory's thoughts with such tenacity. He had known her as child, girl, and woman, and in those years he had never been able to get Eloise Kendall totally out of his mind.

She was like a tune fragment that stuck in a person's brain. Hummed again and again, the fragment would drive one insane until the entire melody was recalled and exorcised.

Except that Gregory could not exorcise Eloise Kendall. Every time he recalled her face, her smile, her spirit, she gained a little more hold on his mind and his heart.

"If you have any charity in your soul," she said, taking his arm and turning him once again toward the door, "you will take me for a drive in that phaeton I see in the carriageway. A very *long* drive."

Though not at all averse to such an expedition, Gregory did not deceive himself by supposing that Eloise had been languishing for his company. "Who wants to murder you now?"

Without batting an eye, she replied, "Everyone."

"Been up to your old tricks, have you?"

"It would seem so. I vow, if I have a friend left on this earth, rest assured it is because I have not seen that person in a twelve-month. In the past twenty-four hours, I seem to have antagonized the entire population of Derbyshire."

Rightly interpreting that to mean she had had words with those few people whose good opinion mattered to her, Gregory knew a moment of hope that he might number among that exalted group.

"Have you a bonnet?" he asked.

At her nod, he bid her get it without delay. "And a shawl. The sun is out, but there is a bit of a breeze. You might become chilled if we drive as far as you wish."

Gregory watched her run up the stairs, her movements agile, yet graceful, and it occurred to him that Eloise might be more fit than the pampered females he was accustomed to. Somehow, the idea appealed to him. Soft, satiny skin over slightly firm muscles. *Umm.*

Heaven help him! He was at it again. If he were not careful, Eloise would return to find him lying dead on the floor, a victim of his own cravat.

Thankfully, no such fate befell him, and when the lady returned a minute or two later, her caller was still able to stand under his own power.

Eloise carried a paisley shawl across her arm, and upon her head she had set a small, chip straw hat with a turned-back brim. Gregory applauded her selection, for a wide poke would not have allowed him to see the wearer's face while they rode.

As they passed through the handsome walnut entrance door, he said, "Name your destination, madam. Shall it be north or south?"

"Please, not the village. I do not wish to see anyone."

"Then north it is."

Gregory had secured the chestnuts to a silent groom that stood several feet from the entrance, so after helping Eloise to the phaeton, he unhooked the leader's harness from the verdigrised statue, then took his

place beside his dark-eyed passenger. The horses were
as eager as the passengers to be on their way, so
within a matter of seconds the travelers were in the
lane, headed north. The low stone wall was to their
right, and to their left, just around a bend in the road,
the entrance to Threwsbury Hall, which the horses
passed by at a steady trot.

Gregory handled the ribbons with real expertise. A
member of the Four-in-Hand Club for years, his driving proficiency was matched by only one or two other
members. Aware of his ability, he never flaunted it or
gave in to the desire to drive at neck or nothing
speeds, and though he paid little attention to such
things, a number of ladies of his acquaintance had
complimented his skill. Not so, Miss Eloise Kendall.

"I feel quite safe riding with you," she said, her
voice dripping with feigned innocence, "for you are
not nearly as cow-handed as I had feared."

Gregory gave her a sidelong look. "Miss Kendall
giveth, and Miss Kendall taketh away."

"Oh," she drawled, "did I say something wrong?"

"No, Miss Saucebox, not if your purpose was to put
me in my place. Tell me, did you come driving with
me just so you could depress any notions I might have
about being a top-sawyer?"

"Are you a top-sawyer?" She batted her eyelashes
like some flirtatious ninnyhammer. "La, sir, I had no
idea. I hope I did not offend your sensibilities."

"Not at all, madam. I promise you, my sensibilities
are never offended by the prattle of impertinent
females."

She chuckled. "I am vastly relieved to hear it."

Gregory stole a moment from his driving to look
into her upturned face. Her eyes were filled with
laughter, and her soft, full lips were parted in a smile,

and all he could think about was how much he wanted to take her in his arms and cover that smiling mouth with his.

But not, of course, in a phaeton traveling down a bumpy country lane at better than five miles per hour! He wanted to kiss her, not do them both permanent damage.

They had traversed at least another quarter mile before Gregory spied a break in the stone wall, and beyond the break a stand of beech trees that looked as though they would provide a suitable place to halt the horses.

As he slowed the team, then turned them to the right and off the lane, Eloise asked him what he was doing.

"I thought we might walk a bit."

"Here? Surely you are not serious."

At the incredulity in her voice, Gregory looked more carefully at the area. Some of the heavy lower branches of the half-dozen beeches touched the ground, very nearly obscuring what lay beyond, but as he stared past the silvery gray bark, he saw the sun's rays reflected on water. "Ah," he said, "a small pond. Famous."

"Famous? I should think *infamous* a more appropriate word."

"Excuse me?"

"The last time you and I were both near a small pond," she said, "*one* of us got decidedly wet."

"Ah, yes. Now you mention it, I do recall a pond and a most unfortunate accident."

"Unfortunate, indeed. For me! Why, I was—"

"Positively the prettiest little girl I had ever seen."

Eloise had meant to take him to task for the dunking that happened eighteen years ago, but at his softly spoken compliment, her wish to rehash the incident evaporated like fog before the sun.

"You wore a lace dress with a pink pinafore," he continued, "and you had a charming sprinkle of freckles across your nose."

"I never!"

While Eloise informed him in no uncertain terms that she had never possessed even one freckle, never mind a sprinkle, Gregory leaped from the phaeton and came around to stand beside her, his arms held out to help her alight. "Come," he said, "let us investigate the pond. If you are a very good girl, I may let you push *me* in this time."

"As tempting as that is," she said, "I must decline the offer."

"Coward," he said.

"Not a bit of it!"

Lifting the hem of her dress, she stretched her foot out so that he could see the cloth slippers she wore. "You told me to get a bonnet and a shawl. You said nothing about boots. As you can imagine, a walk across such rough ground would—"

She got no further, for Gregory ended the discussion by the simple expedient of lifting her down from the phaeton, setting her on her feet, then swooping her up into his arms.

"Gregory! What are you doing?"

"Going to the pond," he replied. "And unless you wish to run the risk of another dunking, I suggest you wrap your arms around my neck and hold tight."

"I will do no such thing."

"Best reconsider that decision," he said, "for I am not as strong as I used to be. If the truth be known, I am growing weaker by the minute."

"All the same, I refuse to—No!"

Gregory had relaxed his arms a fraction, as if he might drop her, and Eloise had screamed. She had also wasted no time in slipping her arms around his broad shoulders.

"Much better," he said.

"Bully."

"Stubborn," he replied, not in the least offended.

Eloise knew he did not need her assistance, for she could feel the bulge of biceps where his arm was wrapped around her waist. Furthermore, held as she was against his rock-hard chest, she could not help but notice the ripple of muscles that brushed against her ribs and the side of her breast.

It was an odd sensation, being held in a man's arms. *No, not odd.* If the truth be known, she found the experience rather exciting. Exhilarating even, for her heart seemed to have picked up its pace and was attempting to *thump* its way free of the confinement of her stays.

"Comfy?" Gregory asked. His warm breath caressed Eloise's cheek, sending a delicious shiver down her spine, and of their own volition, her eyes closed, the better to savor the intoxicating sensation.

She did not answer his question. She dared not speak, for she was certain he would hear in her voice just how disturbed she was by his nearness. Being held so close against him, and knowing he had to be as aware of her body as she was of his, was having an effect upon all her vital organs. First her heart, and now her lungs. With such impediments, Eloise found it difficult to draw sufficient breath.

Gregory did not repeat his question, a circumstance for which Eloise was eternally grateful. Unfortunately, her gratitude was short-lived, for when she opened her eyes and looked into his face—his smug, satisfied face—she knew without question that he was aware of her reaction.

Drat the man! He knew exactly what he was doing. And he knew exactly what it was doing to her!

Overcome by a blend of embarrassment and anger, she said, "I despise you."

"I know," he replied, "and you have every reason to do so. Still, I beg you will put all those reasons aside for a moment."

"And why should I?"

"Because," he said, his voice surprisingly soft and low, "I am leaving tomorrow, and I want to kiss you good-bye."

Chapter Twelve

"What! How dare you ask me to do such a thing."

"I did not ask."

"You did so. You said—"

"I said *I* wanted to kiss you. Kiss me back or not, suit yourself. Though I promise you, a kiss is one of those things that is much better when two people share the experience."

Eloise was engulfed in warmth. "But I . . . I do not wish you to kiss me."

"Yes, you do. I see it in your eyes. Besides, I do it very well. I wager you will like it."

"Why, you . . . you egotistical . . ."

While Eloise tried to think of something vile enough to call him, Gregory tightened the arm that was around her waist, crushing her against him, then he lowered his head and claimed her lips.

Eloise wanted to protest, but the moment Gregory's mouth touched hers, some heretofore unsuspected lethargy invaded her bones, prompting her to cling to him instead, depending upon his strength to sustain her.

It was not a gentle kiss, not at first. Though, truthfully, Eloise suspected she would not have responded half so well had Gregory's firm lips not moved over hers with such eagerness and passion—passion that

sent wave after wave of sensation through her body.
Of their own accord, her arms tightened around his
neck, and as she insinuated her body even closer to
his, awareness of Gregory's strength, his utter male-
ness, brought every inch of her skin to life, causing
her to feel things she had never dreamed of before.

"Eloise," he murmured against her lips. "Beautiful
Eloise. You—"

Yip! Yip! Yip! Yip! Yip!

To Eloise's disappointment, Gregory broke off the
kiss and looked down at the ground, where a whirl-
wind of black-and-white canine sped around his
booted feet, the dog's purpose to discover an unpro-
tected ankle he might bite. "What the deuce!"

"Angus!" Eloise said. "What on earth are you
doing here?"

Perdita's furious little terrier did not respond to the
question; instead, he *yipped* even louder and continued to jump about like something deranged.

"I believe," Gregory answered for him, "the animal
has in mind to save you from the enemy's clutches."

As if Eloise *wished* to be saved! "Angus, you silly
creature. Sit. And be quiet!"

Because the tone of the voice brooked no disobedience, the terrier obeyed, sitting back on his haunches.
When all was quiet, Eloise returned her attention to
Gregory, nuzzling her face against his strong neck, her
actions inviting him to continue where they had left
off.

Gregory pretended not to notice that tantalizing invitation. For his sanity's sake, he had to ignore the
feel of her incredibly soft, silky face against his over-
heated skin.

He had not wanted to stop kissing Eloise—what
man in his right mind would? Unfortunately, if he had

been in his right mind, he would not have kissed her in the first place. It had proved a colossal mistake! The moment his lips touched her, he had realized his error.

Never in a million years would he have guessed that a simple good-bye kiss would turn into the raging fire it had become. For his part, Gregory thanked heaven that the terrier had interrupted them when he did, for that fire had threatened to consume them. He owed the feisty little dog a debt of gratitude for dousing him with a figurative pail of water.

"Actually," Gregory said, feigning a calmness he did not feel, "I do not think Angus is a bit silly. If you ask me, he is a very brave little fellow to tackle a giant who outweighs him a good thirteen stone. Were we more evenly matched, I have no doubt he would be tearing me limb from limb."

Gregory dared not look at Eloise, for at his words he had felt her body stiffen. She had been totally caught up in their kiss, unaware of what her innocent, yet innately passionate response was doing to him. When he ignored her invitation to kiss her again, a feat that had cost him more than she would ever know, he knew she would feel rejected and assume their embrace had meant less to him than it had to her.

What she did not know, of course, was that he should never have lifted her in his arms. Gregory was no green boy; he should have known that such intimate contact with her would be far too dangerous. He should have been aware that holding her soft, pliant body close to his would prove much too tempting.

And he definitely should not have kissed her! Especially not here in this quiet little Eden, where they were totally alone—almost as if they were the only two people on earth—and where anything might have happened.

Vowing to get her home as quickly as possible, before he gave in to the nearly overwhelming desire to take another taste of her soft, sweet lips, Gregory stepped back over to the phaeton and set Eloise on the seat. He did not look at her; instead, he picked up the little terrier and placed the animal on Eloise's lap, then he went around to the other side of the carriage and climbed aboard. After reclaiming the reins, he backed the chestnuts away from the stand of beech trees and turned the pair once again toward the lane.

The return drive was as silent and strained as the original one had been lively, and for the next half hour Gregory gave his attention to the road. He dared not even glance at Eloise, who sat as far away from him as the close seat would allow, her back ramrod straight.

When Gregory turned the horses in at the Deighton Hall carriageway and stopped before the entrance to the dower house, he did not jump down and tie the pair to the silent groom as he had done earlier. This time he remained in the phaeton and merely took the dog from Eloise, then offered her his hand to assist her to alight.

"Eloise," he said, once she was safely on the ground, "I never meant for things to get out of hand. It was entirely my fault, and I apologize. I should have known better than to—"

"No," she said, her voice devoid of all emotion, "it is I who should have known better. After all, this is not the first time you have made sport of me. I promise you, though, it will be the last time."

Having said her piece, Eloise snatched Angus from

Gregory's arms, then turned and hurried into the house, closing the door very softly behind her.

"Damnation!" Gregory muttered, not for the first time since leaving Eloise. "I am surely the biggest fool in nature! Before she merely detested me. Now she hates me. And who can blame her?"

So much for his celebrated finesse with the ladies! And he had thought to give advice to Colin Jamison. *Unbelievable!* "Anyone buying me for an idiot would definitely get his money's worth."

For a member of the Four-in-Hand Club, Gregory was driving like a maniac. Still muttering, and calling himself all manner of names, he had allowed the horses to go from a trot to a gallop and they were moving at too great a speed for a narrow lane.

It was a crazy thing to do, and Gregory knew it, and suddenly the degree of craziness was brought home to him. Just ahead, lumbering along the middle of the lane, was the dun-colored old mare Gregory had passed earlier, and he and the chestnuts were on a collision course with the mare and the dilapidated dogcart.

"Whoa!" he yelled.

"Tarnation!" the man in the brown hat yelled.

While the driver yanked the mare to the left, attempting to get her over to the side of the lane, the little man on the seat beside him began to scream phrases that were half prayer half curses. "Merciful Jasus! Save me."

Though Gregory was grateful for any Divine intervention, he did not wait for it. Using all his skill, and every last ounce of his muscle power, he pulled on the reins, practically pushing his feet through the footboard. "Whoa, boys! Whoa."

The chestnuts took exception to such harsh treatment, of course, tossing their heads and squealing in frightened, high-pitched sounds, but they came to a stop at last, just inches from the swaybacked mare. As for the aged mare, her eyes were rolled back in fear, and she squealed like a pig, but aside from those quite understandable reactions, she was unharmed.

"Go to her head!" Gregory yelled to the little man who was still sending up pleas to heaven.

Apparently accustomed to having orders barked at him, the fellow obeyed instantly, and scurried off the rough board seat to go to the mare. While he calmed the one animal, Gregory leaped from the phaeton and went to the pair. "Hush now," he said, caressing the chestnuts' foreheads and crooning little nonsense words to calm them. "Shh. You have come to no harm. No thanks to me."

Feeling certain he would be obliged to buy his way out of this imbroglio, Gregory was mentally counting the guineas in his pocket, when to his surprise, the driver of the dogcart yelled to his companion to get the mare back into the lane. "And be quick about it."

Once the frightened little man had edged the mare and the small vehicle around the phaeton, the driver yelled, "Let's go!" and cracked his whip above the mare's head.

The mare began to move, and the little man, not waiting for a second order, hurriedly caught hold of the rough seat and swung himself up beside the pale-faced driver.

Within less than a minute, the men, the mare, and the dogcart were well down the lane, moving as quickly as possible, almost as if the driver feared they were being pursued by a band of thieves.

The canvas that had been rolled up and tied to the

seat when Gregory passed the cart earlier had been lowered over the pen space and tied down. It was impossible to see if the cart might now be carrying some valuable hounds. Gregory hoped not, for whatever was hidden beneath the canvas was in for a rough ride.

"Jasus," Lew muttered, his fox face more pinched than usual. "That was 'im. The big fellow from Threwsbury Park. If 'e'd of suspected what we got under the canvas, 'e'd of killed us for sure."

"Shut your mummer," Jack Figby ordered. "If I hear another word from you, I'll kill you myself."

Lew hushed, for he did not take Jack's threats lightly. If it came to it, Lew would rather take his chances with the big fellow who drove the chestnuts than tangle with Jack Figby. Jack was a cold-blooded killer. Human life meant nothing to him—other people's lives, that is.

Jack had dreams of living the good life, and he was certain this job would earn him the money he needed to live the rest of his days in luxury. He had been planning the kidnapping for months, working out every last detail, and for that reason, he wasn't letting anything get in his way. Not Lew, not the big man in the lane, and certainly not the poor kid who was bound and gagged, and stashed in the pen space beneath the canvas.

It was well past five o'clock when Thea knocked at Eloise's bedchamber door. She had heard her cousin come in from her drive, and she had known, somehow, that something was amiss. At that time, however, Thea had been too caught up in her own heartache to wish to investigate. Now, of course, she realized that she had been behaving selfishly. They were a family, and if Eloise was unhappy, it behooved Thea to find out what had happened, and to do what she could to mend the situation.

"Eloise," she called. "May I come in?"

"Enter," came the clipped reply.

Thea had half expected to find her cousin in tears, but to her surprise, Eloise was dry-eyed. Nor had she been crying. She was furious—as furious as Thea had ever seen her. She sat in the window embrasure, her knees drawn up to her chin, and though the pose appeared tranquil enough, Eloise's dark eyes flashed with angry sparks.

"If you value our friendship, Thea, do not ask me any questions."

"But, my dear, I see that you are upset. Perhaps I can be of help."

"You cannot. Help is not possible. When one has been a fool, there is no remedy."

Not sure how to reply to such a remark, Thea said, "In time, perhaps you will—"

"I will still have been a fool."

Eloise closed her eyes and leaned her head against the wall of the embrasure. "I am mortified, Thea, so if there remains in your heart any love for me, allow me this privacy."

Though Thea would have liked to offer what comfort she might, it was obvious her cousin was in no mood for confidences and uplifting words. Not that she blamed her. When one was suffering, what good were words?

Unable to offer help, she suggested that Eloise tidy herself and join her in the morning room for tea.

"I want nothing."

"Be that as it may, you know your brother. Since

he became interested in wrestling, he has become a veritable eating machine. If I know anything of the matter, he has probably been pestering Cook this hour and more, treating her to his impersonation of a starving child."

Eloise smiled for the first time in hours. "Speaking of the poor, fatherless boy, where is he? I have been sitting in this window for some time, and I have not seen him."

"Now you mention it, neither have I."

The smile disappeared, and Eloise swung her feet to the floor. "He should have been home two hours ago. Did he say anything about remaining at Threwsbury Park after his lessons?"

Thea shook her head. "He said nothing to me. But you know boys, they despise having to confide all their plans to us nosy females."

"Nosy or not, I believe I will see if he is in his room."

"You freshen up," Thea said. "I will knock at Jeremy's door."

True to her word, Thea went along the corridor to the boy's room and knocked. There was no answer. "Jeremy?" she called. "Are you ready for your tea?"

When there was still no answer, she turned the knob and opened the door slightly. "Jeremy? Are you there?"

Lew was afraid of high places—always had been—and he found getting up to the cave difficult enough at the best of times. A footpath of sorts led to the big cave, but Jack hadn't thought that place secure enough, so they'd gone higher up the gray cliffs. At that level, there were no real paths, and the unstable shale made it far too easy for a fellow to miss his footing and fall. Not that Jack cared.

Jack Figby cared for nothing and no one but Jack Figby. When he'd halted the mare at the Crags, he'd untied the canvas, taken hold of the large, woolen sack it had concealed, and yanked it and its bulging contents out of the pen space. The sack had fallen to the rough ground with a dull thud—a thud followed by a low moan.

"Haul the boy up to the cave," Jack said, "while I get rid of the mare and the dogcart."

"Haul 'im—" Lew's stomach lurched. "I can't do it, Jack. I'll fall. Carl always did the carrying. The lad's 'alf me weight, and I'm like ter drop 'im."

Jack hadn't said a word. He'd merely looked at Lew with those cold, gray eyes, then he'd touched the knife inside his coat. The threat was there. Spoken or not, it was there, so Lew struggled to set the boy on his feet, then he hoisted him onto his shoulder.

He hadn't been the one to nab the earl's grandson. Jack had seen to that personally, knocking the lad unconscious then tying his hands and feet and stuffing a rag in his mouth to keep him quiet. By the time Lew saw the boy, he was already trussed like a pig, and stuffed into the large woolen bag, an added precaution in case anyone should see them carrying him to or from the dogcart.

It had been Lew's job to take the ransom note and nail it to the stable door. He'd been scared out of his wits, afraid of being that close to the house, but he had done his part. Now, here Jack was making him haul the boy up to the cave. Lew wished Jack had never heard of the Earl of Threwsbury, and he wished he'd never heard of Jack Figby.

Getting up to the cave proved even more difficult

than Lew had feared. The boy was heavy, much heavier than he looked, and twice, while half walking half climbing, Lew had lost his footing and fallen to his knees. Both times he had come close to going over the edge of the cliff, and as a result, his heart had fair jumped out of his chest, and sweat had run down his forehead and into his eyes, nearly blinding him.

The devil only knew what Jack would do to him if he truly dropped the boy. Slit his throat, like as not, and push him over the cliff to join Carl at the bottom of the gorge.

The boy would be lucky if that wasn't his fate, too, once the money was delivered.

Lew couldn't read, so he didn't know what was in the ransom note. All he knew was what Jack had told him; if the earl delivered the money—all ten thousand pounds—the boy would be set free. When they'd met in London to plan the kidnapping, Jack had sworn there'd be no rough stuff, but after what had happened to Carl, Lew wasn't so sure any of them would live to return to town.

After what seemed a month, Lew finally made it to the cave. His knees were scraped and bloody and his back was aching, so he merely leaned sideways and let the woolen sack slip off his shoulder. When the sack hit the floor, the boy inside moaned. "Better not let Jack 'ear you moan again, boy. 'E plays on them as are weak, and it'll go better for you if you try to be brave."

The boy must have heard him, for he made no more sound.

The sun would be going down soon, leaving the cave in total darkness, so Lew found his kit with the spills and the oil of vitriol, and lit the fire. Once the flames took hold, he went over to the woolen sack and untied it. He wouldn't untie the boy, of course, but he saw no reason to make the lad stay inside the sack. Earl's grandson or no, he deserved to breathe. Besides, Jack didn't tell Lew he *couldn't* let the boy out.

He stood the boy upright, so the sack would come off easier, and after he'd pulled it over the boy's head, he led him over to the fire. "You'll be warmer by the fire, lad. This b'aint what an earl's grandson is used ter, but it's all we got. And just in case you got any notions 'bout trying ter escape, best ter forget 'em. Night's coming on, and chances are you'd only get a few feet 'fore you stumbled and fell over the edge. It's a long way down ter the bottom of the gorge."

Lew went to the back of the cave, where he'd left his blanket and the jug of Blue Ruin. He deserved a few pulls after the scares he'd had today. First that big fellow all but running them down, then Jack making him carry the lad up to the cave. And the boy'd been heavy. Much heavier than Lew had expected. Why, he—

Lew stood perfectly still, for a frightening thought had taken hold of him—a thought that caused something vile to rise in his throat, threatening to choke him. "Jasus, save me," he muttered.

His knees began to quake, and he would have fallen to the ground if he hadn't been more afraid of not knowing than of knowing. Slowly, he walked over to the fire, where he'd left the boy. With trembling fingers, he grabbed a fistful of dark brown hair, then tipped the boy's head back so he could get a good look at his face.

"Gorblimey!" he said.

Though his breath was coming in gasps, Lew ran to the mouth of the cave and looked out, checking to see if Jack might be there, eavesdropping as he had done before. Finding no one outside, Lew made his way back to the fire, where he collapsed at last, his legs no longer able to sustain him.

He looked once again at the boy, whose mouth was stuffed with a rag and whose eyes were dulled with fright.

"Boy," he said, "do you want ter live?"

The lad seemed to know exactly why he had asked such a question, and he nodded his head in understanding.

"Then you'd best listen good ter what I tell you. Listen and don't forget. Jack don't know there was two boys, on account of I . . . I forgot to tell 'im. 'E'd kill me for certain if 'e knew I'd forgot. And trust me on this, boy, 'e'll kill you faster'n a bolt of lightning hitting a tree if 'e finds out you b'aint the Earl of Threwsbury's grandson."

Chapter Thirteen

"I will murder him," Eloise said.

After she and Thea had looked all over the house and the grounds, and Jeremy was nowhere to be found, his sister had become concerned—not worried, just concerned. Eleven-year-old boys did not like to hear that their sisters were worried about them; it made them feel they were still in leading strings.

Still, when Eloise found the little caswker, she meant to give him a good piece of her mind. How dare he go someplace without telling anyone. And now, of course, she was obliged to go to the earl's house, where Gregory Ward was still in residence.

Since Gregory was the last person in the world Eloise wished to see, she had searched every place else first. She had even walked to the weir, to see if Jeremy and Basil were there fishing. They were not, nor was there any evidence that they had been there.

Now Eloise had no place left to look except the earl's house.

She knew she must appear a fright, for she had left the dower house without a bonnet or a shawl, and though she had taken a moment to change from slippers to walking boots, she had not expected to travel all the way to the weir and back. She was tired, she was windblown, and her boots and hem were caked with mud from the weir.

The way her day was going, the earl's butler would probably deny her the house!

Unfortunately, she had no such luck.

"Miss Kendall!" the ancient retainer said, the surprise on his face confirming her worst fears about her appearance.

"Is my brother here?" she asked.

"Why, no, miss. At least I do not believe him to be here. Shall I take you to his lordship?"

"No, no. I should not like to disturb the earl. If you would be so kind as to send someone up to the nursery, just to have a look, that would be sufficient."

The butler snapped his fingers and one of the footmen came on the run. "Ask Mr. Browne to step down here," he said. "Inform him that Miss Kendall wishes a word with him."

While the footman ran to the rear of the corridor to use the servants' stairs, the butler offered once again to show Eloise to one of the rooms. "Perhaps I might bring you some refreshment. A cup of tea, perhaps?"

"No, I thank you. I want nothing. And I shall be quite comfortable here in the vestibule."

Having assured the butler that she wanted nothing, Eloise seated herself on a small walnut bench to wait for the tutor. Thankfully, he arrived within a matter of minutes, coming down the front stairs at a run.

"Miss Kendall!" he said, concern on his face. "What is amiss. What brings you here at this time of day?"

What he meant, of course, was what was a young female doing calling at a gentleman's residence when the hostess was away from home. And why was she in such a disheveled state?

Ignoring his question, Eloise rose and went to him. "Is Jeremy here, Mr. Browne? Have you seen him?"

"Why, no. Not since early afternoon. The boys had had a wrestling lesson from Mr. Ward earlier in the day, and they were too excited to settle down to the words of Cicero. Since they were unwilling to concentrate upon their Latin studies, I finally gave up and dismissed them early. Jeremy should have been home by two of the clock."

Eloise had been concerned before, but for some reason, the tutor's words struck fear in her heart. As if she had a premonition of disaster, her knees began to tremble.

"Here," Mr. Browne said, taking her elbow and ushering her back to the walnut bench, "sit down, Miss Kendall. You have gone white as linen."

The butler had remained discretely near at hand, thinking it prudent not to leave an unmarried female and a young man alone in the vestibule, so when he saw Miss Kendall sway, then her face turn quite ashen, as though she might faint, he knew his duty. Without asking permission of her, he hurried to the library to inform his lordship of the young lady's presence.

"My lord," he said, after having scratched at the door and been given permission to enter, "I think you should know, Miss Kendall is here."

To the servant's surprise, his lordship's nephew, Mr. Ward, jumped to his feet, spilling a few drops of his sherry onto the fine old Turkey carpet. "Miss Kendall?" he said. "Here?"

"Yes, sir. She arrived quite five minutes ago, but she would not let me announce her."

Gregory was halfway across the room before the butler could continue. "She asked after Master Jeremy, sir, then she had me send for Mr. Browne."

Gregory paused, forced to tamp down his original surge of excitement.

His first, and obviously erroneous conclusion was that Eloise had forgiven him and come to let him know that all was well between them. Pure wishful thinking, of course. He should have known better. No matter what her reason for being there, however, Gregory could not ignore this opportunity to see her one last time before he left for London. Perhaps she would allow him to explain—

"When Mr. Browne informed her that Master Jeremy was not here," the butler continued, "Miss Kendall swooned."

Swooned! Eloise?

In all the years he had known her, and through all the embarrassing situations he had put her, Eloise Kendall had never fainted. She had too much pride for such girlish tactics. Convinced now that something was very wrong, Gregory flung open the library door and hurried toward the vestibule.

"Eloise," he said, without preamble, "can I be of assistance?"

It spoke volumes that she did not freeze him out as she might easily have done. Instead, she reached her hand out to him. "It is Jeremy," she said. "I cannot find him."

Gregory did not annoy her with platitudes about young boys and their bids for independence; instead, he took her hand and held it in both of his. "Where have you looked?"

"Everywhere." She hesitated, and the blush that stole into her cheeks only emphasized her previous lack of color. "I came here after all else failed."

Gregory was not obtuse enough to question her strategy. He knew exactly why she had left this house for last; she had not wanted to see him. Be that as it may, she had reached out to him now, and he had no intention of spurning that quite magnanimous gesture.

"What would you have me do? Shall I have the grooms saddle up and ride through the neighborhood? I could ride toward the village, while the three from the stables head north, east, and west."

"Would you?" she asked.

"Of course."

When she looked up at him, her lovely brown eyes were filled with moisture, and though no tears fell, Gregory decided he would ride to hell and beyond if it would bring the smile back to her face.

"What is this?" the earl asked, arriving at last in the vestibule. "Surely you cannot think anything has happened to the lad."

He had only just spoken when the footman who had fetched Mr. Browne reappeared. Nervous to have found his employer there, the young servant hung back and merely signaled to the butler. "*Hsst*, Mr. Carswell. Over here, sir."

The butler, affronted at having been summoned by one of his underlings, turned away, ignoring the presumptuous fellow.

"*Hsst*, Mr. Carswell. If you please, sir."

This time the earl turned. "Carswell, what the devil does that fellow mean, hissing like a snake. See to it."

Embarrassed, the butler went to speak with the footman, ready to put a flea in his ear he wouldn't soon forget. Lowering his voice, he said, "How dare you interrupt when his lordship is . . ."

"Sir," the young man said, his neck and ears beet red with embarrassment, "one of the grooms found this letter nailed to the stable door. Since none of the stable lads can read, he brought the letter around to the kitchen and gave it to Cook."

The footman held the cheap, slightly yellowed paper toward the butler. "Cook put it on the kitchen table, which is where I found it just now. It bears his lordship's direction."

Using only his thumb and first finger, the butler took the folded sheet, examining the penciled name and the blob of wax crudely applied to seal the missive. "I cannot think his lordship would be at all interested in anything so—"

"What is that?" Gregory asked, looking directly at the butler.

"It is a letter, sir. It is addressed to his lordship, but I am persuaded he will not wish to read such a—"

"Give it here!" Gregory said.

Acting purely on instinct Gregory snatched the letter from the startled butler's hand, and without asking his uncle's permission, he broke the wax seal and unfolded the single sheet.

We have your grandson. Do just as I say and the boy will come to no harm. Bring sixteen thousand pounds to the Leaping Stag Inn on the Littlefield road. Have it there by Monday.

If you fail to bring the money by that time, I will begin by sending you one of the lad's fingers. A finger will be sent to you each day until I get what I want.

I mean what I say. Do not think otherwise, or it will be the worse for your grandson.

Gregory swore, and though he spoke softly, Eloise heard him. "Is it about Jeremy? Has something happened to him?"

"Wait here," he said, then he thrust the letter into his uncle's hand and ran up the stairs, taking them two at a time.

The earl watched his nephew's peculiar behavior, then he read the letter for himself. Immediately his hand began to shake, and the missive fell to the floor. "The bastards," he said, "they . . . they have my grandson. And they threaten to . . ." He could say no more, for he began to moan, a low, keening sound that sent Eloise immediately to his side.

"Sir," she said, putting her arm around his shoulders, "sit down, I beg of you, before you faint."

"Uncle!" Gregory called from the top of the stairs. "Here is Basil. Safe and sound."

Every head turned to the top of the stairs, where Gregory stood beside Basil, his hand resting on the boy's head."

"My boy!" the earl shouted. "Come here at once."

Basil, apparently sensing his grandfather's distress, ran down the stairs, not stopping until he was kneeling before the frightened man, his hands on his grandfather's trembling ones. "I am safe, Grandfather. I have been in the nursery since early afternoon."

"Thank heaven," the old man muttered, then, "but if you are here, then who . . ." He said no more, merely looked at Eloise, who had bent to retrieve the letter.

"Do not!" Gregory yelled from the stairway. Unfortunately, by the time he reached her, Eloise had read the missive through.

"It is a joke," she said, though the dullness of her voice was enough to convince anyone that she did not believe what she said. "It is some boyish prank. No one would be so cruel. Besides, why would anyone think Jeremy was his lordship's grandson?"

Gregory went directly to her and took the letter from her hand, stuffing it inside his coat where she could no longer see it. Speaking softly, he said, "Whoever wrote the letter must have mistaken Jeremy for Basil, because he was on the grounds."

"But they . . . they said they would cut off his fingers if—"

"Shh. Do not think about what was written in the letter. I am convinced it was but an idle threat meant only to frighten my uncle into taking the kidnappers seriously."

For just a moment, hope shone in Eloise's eyes, but it was replaced on the instant by abject fear. "But Jeremy is not the earl's grandson." She swallowed, for the final horror had only just occurred to her. "Oh, no! Oh, please, no. What will they do to my brother when they discover their error!"

Hoping to comfort her, Gregory said, "Perhaps they need never know."

His lordship, realizing the full implication of the mistaken identity, yelled for his valet. "Greeley," he shouted. "Quick. Pack our bags. My grandson is in danger, and I must get him away from here immediately, before the kidnappers learn of their error and come back for him!"

"Uncle!" Gregory said, horrified at the old man's insensitivity. The earl's nightmare had become Eloise's, and yet the old gentleman seemed unable to think of anything but his own fortunate deliverance.

As it happened, Eloise was too stunned by her own rising fear to notice the earl's totally self-absorbed behavior. "Gregory," she said, her voice little more than a whisper, "what am I to do? I do not have sixteen thousand pounds. Even if Thea and I pooled our funds, we could not raise such a sum."

This time, when her eyes filled with moisture, the tears coursed unheeded down her cheeks. "They will kill my brother," she said. "When I do not deliver the money, the kidnappers will kill Jeremy."

Chapter Fourteen

G regory slept very little, and by daylight he was up and dressed, ready to do all that was necessary to find Jeremy. Not ten minutes after he had returned from driving Eloise to the dower house the night before, he had sent one of his uncle's grooms to London. Riding one of his lordship's fastest horses, the servant took a letter to Gregory's man of business, apprising him of the kidnapping and telling him to send sixteen thousand pounds. Immediately!

"And whatever you do," he instructed the groom, "get that money back here by Monday, without fail. A boy's life depends upon it."

"Yes, sir. I'll not fail."

For what remained of that night, Gregory planned his strategy. After reviewing everything that had happened since he had come to Mansfield Downs, his uncle's suspicions about vagrant ex-soldiers included, Gregory was convinced that the plot to kidnap Basil had been going on right beneath their very noses, and that he had chosen to overlook the signs.

First there was his feeling that something—or someone—had been hidden behind the yews at the gatehouse. Then there was the gatehouse itself; perhaps the intruders there had been of the two-legged variety. Finally, there was the dogcart, and the two men who seemed more like London flash coves than honest country laborers.

Gregory was convinced those two had kidnapped Jeremy Kendall. Any other travelers would have taken advantage of their near accident yesterday to line their pockets. Not so the evasive fellow in the brown hat and the little man who did his bidding. They had fled with all haste. And, of course, hindsight being so accurate, Gregory had little difficulty guessing what—or who—was hidden behind the canvas that covered the pen space beneath the dogcart.

Hoping it would be reasonably easy to follow the path taken by the dogcart, Gregory resolved to see Squire Munson first thing. Munson was Justice of the Peace, and it was through him that anything official could be accomplished. Afterward, Gregory would go to the dower house and bring the ladies up to date.

When he explained the situation to the squire, the middle-aged gentleman was outraged that such a crime could be accomplished in his village, in broad daylight. He was solicitous toward Eloise and the dowager Lady Deighton; unfortunately, he could do nothing official until the criminals were apprehended.

"However," he said, "I've a bailiff who seems to know everything that goes on in Mansfield Downs." He touched his finger to the side of his large, red-veined nose. "Let the wind turn directions, or a bird light on the wrong tree branch, and Fenton knows of it within the hour. What say you, Mr. Ward? Shall I have the fellow sent for?"

Since Gregory was ready to take help from the devil himself, if that was what was needed to restore Jeremy to his grieving sister, he thanked the squire and bid him send for the bailiff at once.

Bert Fenton arrived within a quarter of an hour. He

was a sharp-eyed bag of bones in a faded blue coat and brown breeches, and he was respectful without being obsequious. Gregory liked him immediately.

Fenton listened to the story without interrupting, and once Gregory had revealed all he knew, the bailiff got down to business without any shilly-shallying. "Never seen the two men, sir, strangers both of them, but the dogcart is a different matter."

Gregory breathed sharply, excited to think he might have a lead.

"Nice cart?" Fenton asked, obviously wanting verification of his suspicions. "Or shabby-like?"

"Shabby," Gregory sad.

"Rough plank seat, with space beneath for four medium-sized hounds?"

"That sounds like the one I saw."

"And the horse?"

"A dun-colored mare."

Felton nodded. "I know the rig. Owner hires it out during hunting season."

"Can you give me his direction? I will see what the fellow can tell me about the two men."

When Gregory stood, ready to go to the owner immediately, Bert Felton cleared his throat, the gesture meaningful.

"Yes?"

"Best if I go by myself. No offense, sir, but the owner's like to speak freer if there's naught but me doing the asking."

Taking the bailiff's word for the matter, Gregory reached inside his coat and withdrew a roll of pound notes. "Will he be more inclined to talk, do you think, if we make it worth his while?"

"He'll talk any rood, sir, but if there's a bit of the

ready in his future, he's like not to forget any important details.''

After peeling off several five-pound notes, Gregory
gave them to the bailiff, who stuffed them inside his
coat. "This could take some time, sir. Better if you
let me meet you in, say, two hours. Shall I come to
his lordship's?''

"No, I think not.''

When Gregory left Threwsbury Park an hour ago,
all had been confusion, for his uncle was preparing
for the removal that day of himself, his grandson, and
at least eight male servants whose sole purpose was
to protect Basil while on the road. Unfortunately, the
frightened earl had set the household at sixes and sev-
ens by issuing a set of orders one minute, then coun-
termanding them the next. As well, he had not yet
decided which road to take. North, south, east, or
west, all destinations seemed to him fraught with
danger.

Nothing Gregory said had convinced the old gentleman that his grandson would be safest remaining in
his own home, or that it was unwise to have footmen
standing guard at every door, with fowling pieces
loaded and at the ready. So, rather than risk having
Fenton shot by an overzealous servant, Gregory
thought it best to meet the bailiff at some more public place.

"There is a small posting inn in the village," he said,
"at the top of the high street. I will be there in two
hours. In the taproom.''

"The taproom it is," Fenton said, then he touched
his finger to his forelock in respect and hurried out
though the side door.

After thanking the squire for his help, Gregory rode
over to the dower house to see Eloise, to tell her what

he had discovered so far about the men who had taken her brother. As it turned out, Eloise was not at home, a circumstance that surprised Gregory no end.

"Where is she?" he asked the red-eyed, frightened maid who had answered the door.

"I . . . I can't say, sir."

"Never mind," Thea said. "Thank you, Mary, I will speak to Mr. Ward."

After dismissing the servant, Thea led Gregory into the morning room, where an untouched breakfast tray sat on the round worktable. From the soggy appearance of the toasted bread, and the gelatinous appearance of the basted eggs, the tray had been sitting there for the better part of the morning.

Judging by the dark circles under the lady's eyes and the lines of fatigue around her pretty mouth, she had not slept much the night before. And if the crumpled handkerchief in her hand was anything to go by, she had spent much of the past hours in bouts of weeping.

Gregory held his tongue until the door was closed behind them, then he repeated his question concerning Eloise's whereabouts.

Thea hesitated a few moments before replying. "She has gone up to see Lord and Lady Deighton."

"Perdita? Nonsense! Eloise dislikes the woman. Of what possible comfort would Perdita Deighton be to her."

The dowager Lady Deighton blushed profusely. "My cousin did not go to them seeking comfort. She went to discuss a matter of business."

With so much weighing on his mind, Gregory decided to forsake diplomacy in favor of the direct approach. "What business?"

Even in her distress, Thea took exception to such a presumptuous question. "I cannot say."

"You cannot, or you will not?"

"Gregory, I beg you will not ask me to disclose matters that are between my cousin and me."

His patience was wearing thin, but in deference to the understandable strain both women had been under for the past eighteen hours, Gregory curbed his growing annoyance. "Thea," he said, taking her hands in his, "this is no time to enact me a vignette on family loyalty. Jeremy is missing, and I am doing all I can to insure his safe return."

"You . . . you are? I had no idea."

"Be that as it may, I have made some progress in discovering the identity of the kidnappers, and I came here for no other purpose than to tell Eloise what I have learned so far. Under the circumstances, I feel certain she would like to hear what I have to say."

"Oh, yes," Thea hurried to assure him, "of course she would. You are very good. I did not know you were helping us. Forgive me. I am not myself."

Gregory squeezed her hands, then led her to the gold brocade settee. "Sit," he said, "and tell me why your cousin has gone up to the manor house."

"If you must know, Eloise has gone to ask Lord Deighton to lend her the sixteen thousand pounds the kidnapper demanded for Jeremy's—that is, Basil's safe return."

"Deuce take it! Why would she do that?"

Ignoring the oath, Thea said, "Because she could think of no other course of action."

Gregory swore again.

"Not," Thea continued, a certain hopelessness in her voice, "that I think Lord Deighton will give her the money. Even if he had some sort of family feeling for Jeremy—which he does not—I cannot think the heir is in possession of such an amount. Not unless he had money prior to inheriting Deighton Hall. I know how much the estate provides its owner, and it is nowhere near that large a sum."

"Damnation!" Gregory said. "Why would Eloise turn to Deighton? Is she still so angry with me that she would spurn my offer?"

Angry? Thea stared at him, not certain what to think. "Did you make my cousin some sort of offer?"

"Of course I did. Am I not a human being? Do you think I have no feelings? What man would not have offered?"

Thea could think of any number, but still on shaky ground as to the nature of his offer, she said, "Eloise is beside herself with worry. Perhaps she was in too much distress to heed everything that was said."

"Perhaps."

Apparently only slightly mollified, Gregory stood and began to pace the length of the small room, up and back, then up and back again. "I thought she understood me last evening," he said. "I had hoped to relieve her mind of at least *that* worry."

Thea closed her eyes for an instant, unwilling to let him see the hope she could not hide. When she spoke, her voice was noticeably shaky. "If you please, Gregory, tell me exactly what you told my cousin."

"I told her I would send to town for the money."

"You did?"

"Naturally."

"And . . . and have you done so? Sent for the money, I mean."

He looked slightly affronted. "Of course I did. Last evening. We have only to wait for my uncle's servant to return with it."

To Gregory's dismay, Thea made a strangled sound in her throat, then she hid her face in her hands and began to cry, the intensity of her sobs shaking her shoulders time and again. Unable to watch her in such distress, he returned to the settee and sat beside her, taking her in his arms and allowing her to cry on his shoulder.

After a time, when she had regained some control of her emotions, he gave her his handkerchief. "Dry your eyes," he said, "there's a good girl."

Doing as she was told, she accepted the linen and mopped at the copious tears, but her gaze never left Gregory's face. "I cannot think what to say. Such . . . such a magnanimous act. I do not have sufficient words to thank you for your kindness. Nor, I am persuaded, will Eloise when I tell her. But please, allow me to assure you that no matter how long it takes, my cousin and I will repay every shilling—"

"Repay? Deuce take it, Thea, do not talk such nonsense."

Hoping to change the subject, Gregory told her about going to see the squire, and about enlisting the help of the squire's bailiff.

"Bert Fenton?"

"Yes, do you know him?"

"Only a little. My husband always spoke highly of the man. He is an odd sort of fellow, with a sixth sense about everything that is going on in the neighborhood. No matter what one wishes to know— whether it be when to plant one's wheat, or who is stealing one's poultry—Bert Fenton is the man to ask." She dabbed at the renewed moisture in her eyes. "If Fenton can assist us in finding Jeremy, I shall be in his debt for eternity."

"I believe he will be able to help us, for he seems both observant and resourceful."

Gregory told Thea about the two men he had seen driving the dogcart, and about the bailiff's plan to question the person he believed to be the owner of the cart. "I have a good feeling about Fenton, and I am willing to trust to his instincts."

"As I trust yours, my friend."

There was little more to tell, and just as Gregory came to the end of his story, the tall case clock at the top of the stairs sounded the hour. Standing, he said, "I must leave now, for I am to meet the bailiff at the inn in the village."

"Go," Thea said, standing as well. "I would not detain you from so important a meeting."

She walked him to the entrance door, but before he left, he gave her a message for Eloise. "Tell her I will return once I have spoken with Fenton. And, Thea?"

"Yes?"

"Do not let her go anyplace else. If you must, tie her to a chair and sit on her."

Thea smiled, and Gregory felt certain it was for the first time that day. "I will do as you say," she promised. Then as if only just realizing that it was Saturday, she said, "Speaking of important meetings, I thought you were obliged to leave for London today. Something about an appointment with Lord Liverpool on Monday, to discuss you future."

Gregory did not look directly at her. "I sent a letter of apology to the Prime Minister. It is my hope that he will allow me to meet with him at some later date."

"And if he does not? A slight to the Prime Minister, however unintentional, could mean the end of your political career before it even gets started."

"I know," he said softly, "but some things are more important than one's career."

Thea stared at him for a moment, then to Gregory's surprise, she put her hands on his shoulders, raised up on tiptoes, and placed a kiss on his cheek. "Thank you," she said.

Assuming she was thanking him for his help in searching for her young cousin, Gregory took her hand and lifted it to his lips. "Try not to worry," he said. "We will find Jeremy. You have my word on it."

Gregory was obliged to wait a full twenty minutes in the small, smoky taproom with its low, beamed ceiling and its unmistakable smell of spilled ale and fried meat. A man of action, it went hard with him to sit quietly, staring at a tankard of home brew so thick it might have served as a poultice for a sprained ankle, and listening to the crackle of the fire burning in the large fireplace. At last, when he thought he might be forced to put his fist through the scarred wooden table to calm his impatience, Bert Fenton hurried in, pulled out the chair opposite Gregory's, and sat.

"Out with it," Gregory said, in no mood for polite chitchat. "What did you discover?"

"It's the same dogcart right enough. I gave the owner a couple of fivers, but he was more than willing to talk. Seems the man who did the hiring of the vehicle fits the description of the pale-faced fellow you saw, and besides being as cold-eyed as a fish, he brought the mare back all frothed over and as near blown as makes no difference."

At Gregory's signal, the innkeeper brought over a tankard of ale and set it before Bert, who took a long, grateful swallow. "As you can imagine," he continued after wiping his sleeve across his mouth, "the owner of the cart was tempted to charge the stranger a bit extra for the wear and tear on the animal, but he decided against it when the fellow gave him a look so cold it like to froze his innards."

Encouraged by this information, Gregory mentally crossed his fingers for luck. "Does the man know where the stranger is staying?"

Bert Fenton shook his head. "He didn't ask and the stranger didn't tell."

While Gregory attempted to hide his disappointment, the bailiff said, "For what it's worth, sir, I examined the rig myself."

"And?"

"Inside the pen space, I found a bit of cloth that had caught on the rough board. This is it," he said, removing from his pocket a scrap of cloth no bigger than a shilling. He set the scrap on the table for Gregory to see. "Don't look like clothing to me. More like a piece of a sack, but perhaps it will mean something to Miss Kendall."

Gregory lifted the remnant, examined it without discovering anything from it, then put it inside his coat. "Anything else?"

"Just the cloth, sir, and a sprig of yew."

Yew! Gregory muttered an obscenity. *So, they had waylaid the lad at the gatehouse. Probably jumped out at him from behind the shrubs, the cowards. Grown men overpowering a boy of eleven.*

Gregory's hands balled into fists, and he longed to use them on that pale-faced excuse for a human, the one in the brown hat. *If he has hurt young Jeremy, I swear I will—*

"Also," Bert Fenton continued, "I found a bit of shale lodged in the wheels of the dogcart. 'Course, that's not to say the rock got caught yesterday. Still, there b'aint but one place I know of where there's enough shale to shake a stick at, and the owner says he ain't been there in months."

Trying to keep the excitement from his voice, Gregory said, "And where is that place?"

"Creswell Crags."

"The caves?"

"Yes, sir. And judging by the state the mare was in when the fellow brought her back, I'd say she had traveled at least that far."

"The caves," Gregory repeated. There was a certain logic to using them, for they were accessible, yet far enough from Threwsbury Park not to be the first place a search party would look. "From what I have been told, these men would not be the first to hole up there to avoid detection."

"No, sir, they wouldn't. And there's something else," the bailiff added, "regarding that inn the kidnappers mentioned in the letter, the inn where you are supposed to deliver the money?"

"The Leaping Stag," Gregory said, "on the Littlefield road. Have you news of it?"

Bert nodded. "The owner of the dogcart says the inn's nothing but a den for thieves and the like. And what's more, it's just two or three miles the other side of the Crags."

Chapter Fifteen

Bert Fenton reached inside his coat and removed the remaining pound notes, then laid them on the table in front of Gregory. "Your money, sir."

Gregory pushed the bills back toward the bailiff. "You keep them, Fenton, in appreciation for a job well done."

Bert Fenton shook his head. "I thankee, sir, but I'm not a man as could sleep nights knowing I took money for helping to find a lost lad. Besides, I was thinking we might use that money to hire a couple of swift horses to take us to the Crags."

"Take us?"

"If you'll have me, sir, I'd like to go along. There being two of them, and all."

Gregory gathered up the money, then he offered his hand to the bailiff. "I would be a fool, Fenton, to turn down an offer from a man of your ability."

Bert shook Gregory's hand with all due solemnity, then he suggested they leave within the next hour. "Before it gets too dark to have a bit of a look-see at the Crags. You never know what we might find. Could be the pale-faced fellow left a trail. From what I hear of him, he believes he's got more in his nous box than the rest of us poor mortals. Such people get careless sometimes, for they don't believe anyone else can think a thing through as they have done, and draw the same conclusions."

In perfect agreement with the assessment, Gregory listened carefully to the bailiff's suggestions for finding the men and rescuing young Jeremy. When Bert had finished with his recommendations, Gregory bid him make what arrangements he felt necessary. "I put myself completely in your hands."

Bert did not argue the point. "Shall we meet back here in one hour, sir?"

"I will be here. And, Fenton?"

"Yes, sir?"

"Thank you."

When Eloise finally returned to the dower house, Thea did not need to ask if Lord Deighton had given her the loan; the answer was in the dazed and somewhat desperate look in her cousin's eyes. "What are we to do?" Eloise asked, her voice husky from unshed tears. "I cannot let my brother's fingers—"

"Hush," Thea said. "Do not think of that, my dear. Besides, all is not lost."

"But—"

"Allow me to tell you that Gregory was here. He is gone again now, but he left a message for you."

For just an instant, Eloise seemed to brighten, though the gloom returned rapidly. "I suppose he came to tell me . . . us good-bye."

"No. He is not leaving today."

Thea noted her cousin's sigh of relief, but she did not comment upon it. What was between Eloise and Gregory was just that—between them—and Thea felt it behooved her not to interfere. For that reason, she did not reveal any of her discussion with Gregory about the Prime Minister, nor did she mention the fact that Gregory's decision to forego the meeting and remain here with Eloise might mean the end of his chances for a political career. These were things Eloise needed to discover for herself.

Instead, she said, "Gregory came to let you know that he had sent one of his lordship's grooms to London for the sixteen thousand. He wanted to assure you that the money would be here as speedily as the man could get to town and back."

Eloise merely stared at her cousin. "Gregory did that? For Jeremy?"

"And for you, of course. He said he had told you last evening that he would get the money, but I explained that you had probably been too overcome by shock to hear him."

"He sent for the money? The entire sixteen thousand?"

At Thea's nod of affirmation, Eloise caught hold of the still-open entrance door, her legs suddenly too weak to hold her.

"My dear!" Thea caught hold of her cousin's arm and draped it over her own shoulder. "Come, lean on me and let me help you to the morning room. You look as though you might faint."

"I never faint," Eloise said, but when the walls of the vestibule began to sway in and out, she allowed her cousin to catch her around the waist and lead her to the settee.

After a minute or two of lying with pillows beneath her feet and a wet cloth over her face, Eloise agreed to try Thea's sal volatile. As it transpired, one good sniff from the little blue vial was enough to make the patient sit straight up, the damp cloth falling into her lap. Gasping and trying not to cough, Eloise held both her hands to her temples. "Great heavens, Thea, that witch's concoction is enough to blow a person's head off."

"Or make her sit up," Thea said, a look of relief on her face. "You had grown so pale, I feared you would swoon right there in the vestibule. Thankfully you did not, for had you done so, I would have been obliged to leave you on the floor until Gregory returned to carry you to the settee."

Eloise sat up even straighter, all signs of her previous weakness gone. "Gregory is coming back? When? Can you . . . do you mean today?"

"Within the hour, I should think."

While Thea related all that Gregory had told her about the dogcart and his coming meeting with the squire's bailiff, Eloise began to feel more like her old self. The money was coming, Gregory had not gone to London, leaving her in desperate need of his support, and he and Bert Fenton were investigating a lead to the kidnappers. "Oh, Thea. I pray they are in the right of it, and that we have Jeremy back with us before nightfall."

"I shall say 'amen' to that prayer."

Her spirits lifted by such promising news, Eloise was suddenly all business, and after tossing the damp cloth onto the floor, she rose to her feet. "I must change. Will you help me? I think my habit would be the wisest choice. That way, if I am required to ride, I will be prepared."

"Prepared for what?" asked a masculine voice from the morning room doorway.

"Gregory!"

Both ladies spoke at once, but only one lady's heart began to thump inside her chest as if desirous of getting out. Not that Eloise blamed the foolish organ, for she positively ached to run to Gregory and throw her arms around his neck. With the slightest sign from him—a smile, a wink, an outstretched hand—she would have thrown herself at him, giving herself the pleasure of spilling copious tears all over his waistcoat and bidding him wrap her in his strong embrace.

To her regret, the big oaf did none of those things. He merely stared at her. "Are you ill?" he asked, glancing toward the sal volatile Thea still held.

Eloise brushed the question aside with an impatient wave of her hand. "I beg of you, do not worry about me. Instead, tell me what you have discovered."

He lost no time in relating everything the bailiff had told him, as well as their plans to ride to Creswell Crags. "Do you recognize this?" he asked, showing her the scrap of cloth.

She shook her head. "Why? Is it important?"

"I had hoped you might identify it as belonging to Jeremy. It would have confirmed my own belief that he was taken away in the dogcart. However, I am not discouraged, for my instincts tell me that the men I saw are the kidnappers."

"Of course they are," Thea said. "You were a soldier long enough to learn to listen to your instincts. And I, for one, would be willing to follow you into battle."

"As would I," Eloise agreed. "As it happens, I was on my way to my room to change into my habit when you arrived. If you will allow me five minutes to change, I shall then be ready to go wherever you say."

"Excellent," Gregory replied, "for I say you remain here with your cousin, where no harm will befall you."

"But I want to go with you. I must find my brother."

Gregory could not believe his ears. "This is foolish beyond permission, Eloise, even for you. You are pluck to the backbone, no one who knows you can doubt that, but you have no business riding to the Crags with Fenton and me."

"And why not, I should like to know?"

"Because," he replied, "we will do much better if we are not required to see to a lady's comfort."

"Comfort! As if I cared for that when my brother may be grievously injured. Can you not see that it is impossible for me to remain here walking the floor and wringing my hands while Jeremy may have need of me."

"And can you not see that you would be a hindrance to the bailiff and me?"

"I would not!"

They argued for several minutes, with Thea excusing herself tactfully to fetch something for Gregory to eat—something to sustain him through what might prove to be a long day. She was only just returning to the morning room when Eloise ran past her and hurried up the stairs. Naturally, Gregory thought Eloise's purpose in leaving was to throw herself onto her bed and give in to a much-deserved bout of tears, but in this he misjudged his woman.

Five minutes later, after making short work of two cups of tea and a cold roast beef sandwich, Gregory bid Thea not to let Eloise cry for too long. With her assurance that she would see to her cousin, he went outside, untied his horse from the silent groom, and prepared to mount.

He had only just thrown his leg over his horse when Eloise exited the house. She was dressed in her serviceable green faille and a pair of no-nonsense riding boots, and she came directly to him, her arm raised. "Give me a hand up," she said. "I can ride behind you until we reach the village. Once we get to the inn, you may hire me a sturdy horse for the ride to Creswell Crags.''

"No! Absolutely not. I forbid it," he said, the tone of his voice brooking no disobedience. It was a tone he had used to good effect many times with young subalterns, making them quake in their boots.

Unfortunately, Eloise had never been in the cavalry, and she did not tremble before his wrath. "If you refuse me," she said, her own voice surprisingly calm, "I shall walk to the village. Once there, I will hire my own horse and ride alone to the Crags.''

Gregory looked into her upturned face for what seemed like hours. No one had to tell him that she was frightened for her brother, or that she wanted to help find the lad, and as much as he hated having to deny her, that was the only wise course of action. "Forgive me," he said softly.

Though it broke his heart to do it, Gregory turned his horse and rode down the carriageway, leaving Eloise standing beside the silent groom. He did not look back. He dared not!

Gregory and Bert Fenton had galloped their horses the final mile of their journey. The sun was beginning to set, and though neither man spoke his thoughts, they both understood the difficulties darkness would add to their search. Making the slow, somewhat arduous walk up the rough footpath that gave access to the caves would be difficult enough in the dark, but without sufficient light, it would be impossible to follow the kidnappers' trail.

The narrow gorge known as the Crags appeared to stretch for miles to the north and to the south, and it contained who-knew-how-many dozen caves. Without some sort of clue where to start looking, they could spend all night searching and still not find the boy.

Since they were in agreement that the men with the dogcart would not wish to be seen, and therefore would not have chosen to ride to the relatively flat meadow where visitors left their horses, Gregory and the bailiff did not bother going there. Instead, they turned their horses onto an overgrown footpath that led around to a more dangerous, ergo, mostly unused, access to the gray cliffs.

While Gregory tied the horses to a smallish larch, one of the few trees that grew on this side of the gorge, Bert went immediately to work, getting down on all fours so he would not miss the tiniest detail. "Here, sir," he called. "Have a look."

Gregory hurried over to where the bailiff's bony rump stuck up in the air. Bert had been rummaging in a pile of loose rocks and shale, and he had something in his hand.

Please, God, let it be another piece of that black woolen.

"What is it? What have you found?"

"This," he replied. He held his hand open, palm up, to reveal a still-green sprig of yew tree.

Lew Rolf was so hungry his gut thought his throat'd been cut. For a small man, he needed an uncommon amount of food, and since he'd begun this job, he seemed never to have a full belly. He'd plucked the last of the scrawny chickens and skewered it, then held the stick over the fire for fully twenty minutes. And still the stupid fowl refused to brown. He was about to give up and eat the thing half cooked, when Jack Figby suddenly stood and walked over to the mouth of the cave.

"Shh," Jack said, stepping back into the shadows to the right of the mouth.

Since the boy lay at the back of the cave, still tied and gagged, Lew knew the order was meant for him. Though why he should be quiet, he couldn't say. He'd been at this gorge for the better part of a month, and no one had ever ventured this far up. Still, he knew better than to cross Jack. The man was acting crazier by the hour, and the last thing Lew wanted was another confrontation.

The *next* to last thing he wanted was to lose that chicken, so he set it on the ground beside him where it would not burn if Jack should tell him to do something. He could brush the dirt off his food, but he couldn't eat it if it was charred to a cinder. As for Jack, he hadn't eaten a bite since they brought the boy up yesterday. Every so often he'd taken a swig from a vial he kept in his pocket. Lew suspected it was laudanum, which would explain Jack's growing belief that everyone was bent on betraying him and taking what was rightfully his.

"Stay where you are," Jack ordered. "Somebody's coming."

Lew didn't hear anything, but then he hadn't been living off laudanum for close to forty hours. He remained where he was, though, for Jack had his knife in his hand, the long, slim blade already unfolded from the handle.

"Turn around, fool," Jack whispered. "Show 'em your back. You want 'em to know we heard 'em?"

Lew began to tremble. He wanted to get out of the light and hide in the shadows like Jack was doing. If someone truly was coming, anyone sitting by the fire was an unmissable target.

What if they had a pistol!

Tears slipped down Lew's scraggly face. This was the way his life always seemed to go. There was never a good choice. Oh, no. He always had to choose between something like this—sitting in the firclight and waiting to be shot, or hiding and waiting for Jack to find him and slit his throat for not obeying orders.

He heard the footsteps only moments before the two men appeared at the mouth of the cave. The first one he recognized; it was that big fellow who'd been teaching the boys how to wrestle. The second one, a bag of bones on feet, he'd never seen before.

"Do not move," the big man said, "or I promise you, I will shoot you like the mad dog you are." To his companion, he said, "Go to the lad while I watch this one."

The skinny fellow had just stepped inside the cave when Jack reached out and grabbed him from behind, wrapping his arm around the fellow's throat. He stuck the point of his knife into the man's chest, pushing just hard enough for a bit of red to show along the front of the captive's shirt.

"The big fellow's got a saddle pistol," Lew yelled.

"Drop it," Jack said, "and come inside. Keep your hands where I can see them, or your friend here is a dead man."

When the big man hesitated, Lew said, " 'E means it, Jack does. 'E's already killed one man. Lying at the bottom of the gorge, Carl is, with 'is throat cut from ear ter ear."

"Shut your mummer," Jack said.

The big man was still weighing his options when the kidnapped boy moaned. "Jeremy?" he said, staring inside the cave, straining to see the boy's face in the shadows at the very back. "Are you all right, lad?"

"The boy's in good health at the moment," Jack

said. "Come in and see for yourself. Or stay out there if you want to, and I'll throw him out to you, piece at a time."

The big man swore, then he tossed the pistol behind him, so that it landed in the shale outside the cave. "I am coming in," he said, then he ducked to keep from hitting his head. Once he was inside, Jack slammed the skinny fellow against the rock wall and let him fall to the ground, unconscious.

Jack came out of the shadows to get a good look at the big fellow. "Well, Mr. London Toff, we meet again." He was sort of twirling the knife around in his fingers, as if toying with the big fellow and sizing him up at the same time. As he stepped closer and closer, he smiled.

"I don't like you," he said. "I don't like any of you fine *gentlemen*, always looking down your noses at me. Well, you won't be looking down it much longer, for I mean to kill you."

"Really?" the big man asked, not the least sign of fear in his voice. "It may surprise you to discover that I do not kill all that easily."

The whole time Jack had been coming closer and closer, the big fellow had been standing his ground. Now, with Jack no more than arm's length away, he moved sideways, forcing Jack to do the same.

" 'E's going ter try to wrestle you down, Jack. Don't let 'im. 'E knows all the moves."

"No," the big man said, "I think I will do it his way."

Quick as lightning, he reached inside his coat and pulled out a knife, and for once Jack looked surprised, even a bit frightened. But not for long, for Jack didn't believe that anyone could best him.

The two men never took their eyes off one another.

Slowly, cautiously they circled around, each one trying to swipe the other with his knife, without either of them doing more than slicing up each other's coat sleeves. Finally, the big man lunged forward and got a chunk of Jack's arm, drawing blood at last, but when he straightened and stepped back, he stumbled over the skewered chicken Lew had set on the ground for safe keeping.

"What the . . ."

The words had no sooner left his mouth than his foot slipped out from under him and he pitched backward to the ground. Immediately Jack lunged forward, his knife raised and ready to plunge into the big man's chest. Before he got the chance, however, the big man locked both his booted feet around Jack's ankles, then rolled over onto his right side, causing Jack to fall.

"Hey!" Jack shouted, as if to complain that his opponet had not played fair.

In less time than it took to figure out what the big man had done, he was on top of Jack, his forearm pressed against Jack's windpipe, pushing and pushing. Jack thrashed about like a banked fish, his only sound a gasping noise. His pale face was turning redder by the second, and if Lew knew anything of the matter, Jack was about a minute away from joining old Lucifer down in hell.

Lew wouldn't be a bit sorry to see Jack Figby dead. He could spend eternity tending the fires, for all Lew cared. He'd more than earned his fiery reward. But once Jack was gone, how would Lew defend himself against the big man?

Figuring he'd be the next to have his gullet squeezed to pulp, Lew picked up a piece of firewood and raised it over the big man's head. He was no killer, but a fellow had to do what he could to stay alive. Just as he started to bring the wood down across the man's broad neck, Lew heard a scream.

"No!" someone shouted.

Immediately afterward, a pistol exploded, the echo inside the small space nearly deafening Lew. An instant later, his left foot seemed to catch fire. Dazed, he dropped the firewood and looked down. His shoe was all torn up, and blood gushed from inside the smoking leather.

"Jasus save me!" he cried, plopping down on the dirty floor and cradling his injured foot. "Why'd you have to shoot me?"

"I'll shoot you again," the woman said, "if you move so much as an inch. And this time, I'll not miss your head."

Chapter Sixteen

"She was aiming at his head," Jeremy said, laughing so hard he nearly fell off the settee, "and she got him in the foot."

Enjoying the joke at his sister's expense, the young boy told the story of the shooting for the fifth time. This time, his audience was his friend, Basil Threwsbury, who had arrived shortly after the vicar and his wife had congratulated Jeremy on his narrow escape and then said their good-byes.

"You should have been there," Jeremy said, growing braver with each hour he spent in his own home, "your cousin Gregory got a footlock on the ankles of the man called Jack, then he rolled to his right, flipping Jack over like he weighed no more than a newborn kitten. It was something to see."

Basil stared, his mouth hanging open in amazement. "Blimey!" After looking around to assure himself that none of the ladies had heard him swear, he said, "What happened next?"

"Then, quicker than you can say Bob's your uncle, your cousin was on top of the man, squeezing the life right out of him."

"Wow! Sure wish I had been there to see it. You have all the luck."

"Well," Jeremy said quietly, "it was pretty scary, actually. I was never so glad to see anyone as I was to see your cousin Gregory and the squire's bailiff. The bailiff's arm is broken, by the way. Did you see him leaving as you came in?"

Basil shook his head. "I saw no one other than Miss Kendall. She was walking toward the brook and the little arched bridge. I called to her, but she must not have heard me. Probably embarrassed, knowing you would tell me what a poor shot she was." He laughed again. "Aimed at his head and got him in the foot! Don't know when I have heard anything quite so funny."

"She's a female," Jeremy said, as if that explained it all.

While Jeremy started from the beginning, retelling his version of the kidnapping and the rescue story, his sister strolled toward the brook, trying desperately to erase the entire incident from her memory. She would have considered herself the luckiest of women if she had awakened this morning without a single recollection of the last two days.

There was her lone ride to Creswell Crags, her hazardous and quite frightening climb over the slippery shale, and especially the sight of that horrid little man about to bash Gregory over the head with a piece of firewood. What sane person would ever want to call those to mind?

As for shooting the little man, Eloise was not proud of that. But she would do it again!

If she possessed a magic wand—one that would allow her to expunge every memory beginning with the ransom letter—she would use that wand now, choosing to remember only one thing about the entire incident. She would never forget the utter joy of finding her brother alive and unharmed—with all his fingers and toes intact—and the marvelous feel of him running into her waiting arms.

For a veritable age, their tears had mingled as the eleven-year-old had allowed his sister to hold him as she used to do when he was a little boy. He had held her as well, squeezing her so tight she thought he would never let her go. Even on the long ride home, when he had shared her horse, Jeremy had clung to her, and once during the too-short night, he had come and knocked at her bedchamber door, asking if he could sit on the foot of her bed like he used to.

She had bid him come in, and brother and sister had spent what remained of the night recalling happy times with their parents. Every sentence began with "Do you remember the time," and neither of them wished to ruin the happy recollections with talk of Creswell Crags and the kidnappers.

There would be a trial, of course; it could not be avoided. Gregory was convinced the kidnappers would be convicted without either Jeremy or Eloise being obliged to testify, and he gave it as his opinion that the malefactors would probably be transported to the penal colony in Australia.

Eloise had read somewhere that Australia was a wild, dangerous place. She hoped it was true. Never mind the good vicar's advice that she should find it in her heart to forgive the kidnappers. She could not do so. How could she forgive two grown men for threatening the life of an innocent boy?

She had only just reached the bridge when she heard the sound of galloping hooves. Hoping it might be Gregory, she stopped, ready to return to the carriageway to meet him.

To her surprise, the rider was not Gregory. The slim gentleman astride the lathered and winded horse was darker than Gregory, and his gray coat was liberally caked in mud, as though he had ridden long and hard, without once stopping to refresh himself.

He rode right up to the dower house, and after alighting, he unstrapped a bulging saddlebag, slung it onto his shoulder, then hurried to the door. Before he had an opportunity to knock, however, the door was thrown open.

Thea stood before him, a smile trembling upon her lips, "Colin," she said.

"My dearest love," he replied. "I came as soon as I heard. I have brought the sixteen thousand, and I promise you, I will not leave here until the boy is found and returned to you and his sister."

"Colin," Thea said once again, then words seemed to fail her. With a noise that was not quite cry, not quite laugh, she walked directly into Colin Jamison's arms and kissed him full on the lips.

Eloise watched unashamedly as the two lovers kissed and kissed again, apparently unable to slake their thirst for one other. She was happy that Colin had returned. Thea loved him and he loved her, and they deserved to be together. She wished them nothing but happiness.

That was, of course, exactly what she wished for herself. Unfortunately, she felt certain such happiness would never be hers. She loved Gregory Ward, loved him with all her heart, with all her soul, and with all her mind, and loving him as she did, she knew that no other man could ever take his place.

If only he loved her just a little. Sadly, he did not, and now Eloise could not think what to do. When she let Gregory kiss her with such devastating passion, and returned his kisses, not even trying to hide her response to him, she had crossed the line. There was no going back. Never again could she hide behind a pretense of disliking him.

Not that she wanted to pretend such a thing, especially not when she owed him so much. Gregory had risked his life, not to mention his career, to rescue her brother, and she would be eternally grateful to him. "And I am grateful, genuinely so."

"If you are talking to me," Gregory said, startling her into a gasp, "you can keep you damned gratitude. I want none of it."

Somehow he had crossed the bridge without her hearing his approach, and now, surprised by his vehemence, Eloise said, "I see you are still angry with me. Was I such a nuisance?"

"Yes. No." He muttered something beneath his breath, then he said, "You know you were not a nuisance. Far from it. Had you not come along when you did, my brains would now be splattered all over the floor of that cave."

Eloise shuddered. "I beg of you, do not say such things."

"Very well, but allow me to tell you that I was wrong to refuse to take you with me. You had every right to be there."

When she said nothing, he added, "And, being the noble fellow I am, I have come here so that you may watch me eat my words."

He pretended to sprinkle salt over an imaginary object, then feigned taking a large bite. "Mmm. Crow. Very tasty."

She knew he was trying to make her laugh, but she could not do so.

"Ah," he said, "I believe it is you who is still angry with me."

She knew to what he referred; the afternoon two days ago when he had taken her for a ride in his phaeton, then lifted her in his arms and kissed her.

He had kissed her until her heart melted inside her, then he had pushed her away. "I was angry," she said. "But no more. How can I be angry with the man who rescued my brother."

"And how can I be angry with the lady who saved my life."

"Easily," Eloise said. "Just let us remain in one another's company for five minutes, and I will surely do something to give you a disgust of me."

"A disgust of you!" Gregory stared at her, surprise in his green eyes. "My dear Eloise, you could not be more wrong."

"Liar."

"No, really. When have I ever by word or deed given you to believe that I took you in disgust?"

Again Eloise's thoughts went to the ride, but embarrassment kept her silent.

He searched her face, seeking the answer to something, Eloise was not sure what. "I believe," he said, "that you and I are long overdue for a talk—a serious talk."

A serious talk. Was he toying with her again? Twice before Eloise had let her imagination run away with her, and if she was to retain even a shred of self-respect, she had better be quite certain this time of Gregory's intentions.

"Very well," she said, "a serious talk it shall be. You may go first."

"Au contraire," he said, "a gentleman should always allow a lady to—"

"No, no. This was your idea, Gregory Ward, and if you say ladies first, I vow I will push you into the brook."

"If it will make you happy, sweetings, you are welcome to try."

Sweetings. There he was, toying with her again, and

too furious to think straight, Eloise ran directly at him. She might as well have tried to push over a brick wall, for Gregory did not even sway under her attack.

What he did was catch her around the waist, lift her off the ground, and swing her around. When he stopped, he did not set her down, but held her with one arm, her soft body pressed against the length of his. Crushed against him as she was, Eloise was aware of every muscle, every hard, masculine plane of his physique, and the feel of him was doing strange things to her breathing.

She did not struggle to break out of his embrace, and encouraged by this, Gregory put his free hand beneath her chin and lifted her face where he could look deeply into her eyes. His own eyes darkened, and the seriousness of his expression set Eloise's pulse to racing.

After a few seconds she slipped her arms around his neck, and he rewarded her show of amiability by brushing his lips ever so gently across hers. It was a kiss of infinite tenderness, and it made Eloise's heart sing. She wanted him to kiss her again, but he seemed bent on conversation.

"Do you know," he said, "I think I have loved you since the first day I ever saw you."

Eloise swallowed. "You love me?"

Ignoring her question, he said, "You were dressed in your little lace dress with the pink pinafore, and you looked like a fairy princess."

Eloise's heart was beating so hard she thought the noise might bring Thea and Colin from the house. Thankfully it did not, for she wanted to be alone with Gregory. Could he mean what he had said? Had he loved her all those years? "And I suppose you would have me believe that you fell in love with me when you saw me all covered over in mud and pond scum."

Gregory chuckled. "Not that you do not look perfectly charming in pond scum, my sweet, but it was later that I knew my heart. I pulled you out of the water and you kicked me in the shins, and I knew then that we were meant for each other."

"But every time we are together, some disaster happens."

"True," he said. "Every time I am near you, you wreak havoc with my heart, and I wreak havoc with your person. And since I cannot risk waiting for some meeting where neither of us is at outs with the other, I have decided to put my luck to the test."

Eloise's breath caught in her throat. "Your luck?" she said.

He placed another of those soft, tender kisses on her lips. "Eloise Kendall," he said, "will you marry me?"

Yes, yes!

When she could not draw sufficient breath to get the words out, she let her actions speak for her. Giving a tug on his muscular neck, she encouraged him to bend sufficiently for her to press her lips against his.

At first Gregory did not help her, merely let her kiss him as she would, but after a minute, he moaned against her mouth, then he crushed her so close against him she felt the beat of his heart mingle with her own.

Warmth spread throughout her body, and as his lips moved back and forth across hers, tasting, teasing her own until she thought she would go mad with longing, the warmth became a raging fire. Then, blessedly, Gregory deepened the kiss, putting her out of her misery.

Eloise had never known that such pleasure, such passion existed, and as she responded to the man she loved, giving him freely of her heart, he murmured words of love against her mouth, her hair, her eyes.

"You have not answered my question," he said at last. "Will you be my wife?"

"Yes," she said, "I will marry you."

They sat on the bank of the brook, near the bright pink phlox, and planned their life together. If this was not heaven, it was close enough to suit Eloise. What bliss to sit in this lovely spot, with Gregory's arms around her, knowing she could kiss him anytime she wished . . . tell him she loved him as often as it pleased her . . . ask him to say the sweet words once again to her.

They had remained in one another's arms for the better part of an hour, when Thea came to the door of the dower house and called Eloise's name.

"Yes?" she replied.

"Come in, if you please, my dear. I have an announcement I believe you will be pleased to hear."

Since Gregory and Eloise had an announcement of their own, he sprang to his feet and reached down to take her hands. "Come my love," he said.

As he pulled her to her feet, there was the unmistakable sound of ripping material.

"Uh oh," he said. "Tell me I was not standing on your skirt again."

Eloise did not need to look behind her, for a gentle breeze cooled her bare ankles, telling her all she needed to know. "Gregory, my big, wonderful oaf, I can see now that we will spend a fortune on dress repair."

After giving her a smile so wicked it stole her breath away, Gregory took her in his arms again and kissed her, promising that the next time he made a mess of her clothes, it would be on their wedding night. "And I promise you," he whispered, "you will not mind at all."